SAN DIEGO PUBLIC LIBRARY

3 1336 03164 8067

P9-CJS-837

32x (7/95-1/00) [2/00]

40X 1/03 4/03
45X (7/10) 5/11
47X (11/13) 10/14

SK

SAN DIEGO PUBLIC LIBRARY

SAN DIEGO PUBLIC LIBRARY
SKYLINE HILLS

**ALWAYS BRING YOUR
CARD WITH YOU.**

JUL 2 1 1993   GAYLORD

A Fit of Shivers

A Fit of Shivers

Tales for Late at Night

JOAN AIKEN

SAN DIEGO PUBLIC LIBRARY
SKYLINE HILLS

Delacorte Press

JUL 2 1 1993

3 1336 03164 8067

Published by
Delacorte Press

Bantam Doubleday Dell Publishing Group, Inc.
666 Fifth Avenue
New York, New York 10103

This work was first published in Great Britain in 1990
by Victor Gollancz Ltd.

Copyright © Joan Aiken Enterprises Ltd. 1990

All rights reserved. No part of this book may be reproduced or
transmitted in any form or by any means, electronic or
mechanical, including photocopying, recording, or by any
information storage and retrieval system, without the written
permission of the Publisher, except where permitted by law.

The trademark Delacorte Press® is registered in the U.S. Patent
and Trademark Office.

Library of Congress Cataloging in Publication Data

Aiken, Joan, [date of birth]
    A fit of shivers : tales for late at night / Joan Aiken.
        p. cm.
    Summary: Ten short stories with elements of horror or the
supernatural, including "The L-shaped Grave," "The
Shrieking Door," and "Watkyn, Comma."
    ISBN 0-385-30691-1
    1. Horror tales, English. [1. Horror stories. 2. Short
stories.] I. Title.
PZ7.A2695Fl   1992
[Fic]—dc20   92-6130
                                                        CIP
                                                        AC

Manufactured in the United States of America

October 1992

10 9 8 7 6 5 4 3 2 1

BVG

A Fit of Shivers

Contents

Number Four, Bowstring Lane

IN CROWBRIDGE, a small town not far from the English Channel, the boards of estate agents blossom like hollyhocks among the pointed red roofs, the Tudor chimney pots, the pantiles, wrought-ironwork, and cobbled walks. Crowbridge, so cute, so gracious, so full of raftered pubs and gate-legged tables, boasts more retired gentry per square foot of ground than any other borough in southeast England; it also possesses more ghosts. Nearly every diamond-paned cottage claims to have been occupied, at one time or another, by some historical character of note or notoriety; and, dying, whether respectably or amid scenes of drama and scandal (for Crowbridge, full of urban virtue and sobriety now, has known its fair share of skulduggery and crime)—dying, the former residents conferred a legacy of perturbed spirits who moan, squeak, gibber, jabber, rap, rattle, clank, wail, keen, and scrabble every night and all night, beginning promptly at midnight and keeping up their cacophonous chorus until the formal signal of

cock-crow calls a sudden halt to the racket. (Fortunately Crowbridge is a very compact little conurbation
with green marshes encircling its ancient walls; farms
equipped with veritable roosters lie within earshot of
the townspeople in their neat houses.)

The death rate among the inhabitants of Crowbridge is unusually high; not from disturbed nights or
lack of sleep (they all wear earplugs), nor due to any
insalubrity of the locality or climate (indeed Crowbridge is billed as one of the healthiest burghs in southeast England), but simply because most of the house-
holders are senior citizens of ample means who retire to
pass their declining days in this peaceful and picturesque spot; the actual number of declining days not infrequently proves to be a great deal less than the quality, and often some elderly nabob has done little more
than decorate his dwelling to his own taste and plant a
few bulbs in the garden before natural mortality carries
him off and his demesne is once again on the market, of
course at an increased price; house agents turn over a
rapid business here, and seven of them have large,
handsomely furnished offices in the High Street, while
another nine occupy ex-market stalls and smaller infe-
rior premises in Station Approach.

It was to one of these lesser offices that Marcus
Fantail repaired on a Saturday morning, having reached
Crowbridge for the first time by train. Travel by public
transport was a complete novelty to Marcus, and so
was the prospect of early retirement from his well-es-
tablished position in television. An unsuspected affliction of the heart, making its unwelcome presence
known by severe and sudden chest pains, had brought
his professional life to an abrupt close. For twelve years
he had been one of the best-known names in the busi-

ness, controlling a wide spectrum of popular and successful drama programs. He was a big, jolly man, his face well known both on screen and in the press. The best-known of his programs, *A Phantom at the Fireside*, a series of half-hour humorous ghost plays, had been running, to wide acclaim and impressive ratings, for the last eight years.

It was a natural progression, therefore, that Marcus, having gone through the regular list of amenities—up-to-date fitted kitchen with tiles and dresser, central heat, paved garden, two-bath, four-bedroom, garage, and dining room—should inquire concerning the cottage he was proposing to purchase:

"And of course it has a ghost?"

Young Mr. Teazel, of Teazel and Gritchby, appeared a little embarrassed.

"Well, sir, I'm afraid, at this present moment in time that, no, just now it does not have one. But that might possibly be a matter of arrangement."

(It was taken as a matter of course that intending purchasers of house property in Crowbridge would prefer and expect the property to be haunted; that the premises should be shared with some ghostly resident was a desideratum; in fact properties lacking this amenity were rated lower, priced lower, and their owners shared a similarly humble place in the social rating of the town.)

"That," explained young Mr. Teazel, allowing a slightly condescending note to enter his voice, "is why the little property is available on such favorable terms. You would not find another in Crowbridge, I assure you, Mr. Fantail, at anything like this price. It is"—he lowered his voice still further—"a steal. But why not stroll around and have a look at it, sir? It is a most attractive little place, I assure you."

Selecting a bunch of keys from a large board, Mr. Teazel led his client out, along the wide station approach, pleasantly bordered with pollarded limes, along Wharf Way, up Dolphin Passage, with its cobbles and bow windows, through a narrow alley known as the Spindles, which smelled of coffee from all the little tea places that graced its length, and so into Bowstring Lane, where four brick-and-tile cottages with neat front gardens faced out across a short, broad footway and a low stone parapet on to a wide vista of green marshland terminating in a silvery line of distant sea.

"Delightful prospect southward, as you see, Mr. Fantail," said Mr. Teazel, throwing open one of the neat front gates and fitting a fine new Chubb key into a shining new lock in the ancient oaken door. "The garden requires only minimal upkeep, an advantage for a gentleman in your—er—state of health, sir, and the rest of the premises are in first-rate condition, having been recently redecorated."

Marcus could see that this was so. The little house was pristine: windows fitted, plumbing worked, paint gleamed, glass shone, and all the electrical equipment appeared to have been newly installed.

"The last owner had not—been here very long?" he suggested.

"Lord Woolsack, sir, a most distinguished old gentleman, we are handling the property on behalf of his grandchildren," divulged Mr. Teazel, shaking his head. "Aged ninety-two when he retired from the bench, hardly had time to do more than plant a few pansies in the window boxes when *Anno Domini* caught up with him. Sad, very sad. He really loved the little house. But he had left it so late. Now, you, sir . . ."

Tact brought him to a halt for a moment, then he began again. "You, sir, still in your fifties, will surely have plenty of time to enjoy living in Crowbridge," he said kindly.

"Lord Woolsack, then, did not object to the lack of a ghost?" inquired Marcus, casting his eye up a definitively Tudor, but well-swept chimney.

"Why, no, sir. He said that he had enough memories of shady deeds and wicked goings-on from his years in court; he made no complaint. And, of course, a gentleman of his standing would be certain to find a sufficiently eminent place in the society of the town—if he wished it—without the need for, as it were, supernatural assistance."

Mr. Teazel here paused again delicately. Both he and his client were quite aware that television, though undeniably well paid and ranking foremost among callings conspicuous in the public eye, did not by any means command such a high place on the scale of social values then obtaining in Crowbridge; in fact it cut very little ice, ranking as grocery might have done a hundred years earlier. To be a TV executive in Crowbridge was to be graded little better than a plumber; unless you possessed some other asset.

"You said something before," recalled Marcus, withdrawing his head from the chimney. "About a ghost. Not at present, you said, but it might be subject to arrangement. What did you mean by that?"

"Why, sir, there is a lady, a Mrs. Spearpoint, a long-standing resident in the town, who is, who finds herself able to supply such deficiencies. More or less to the customer's requirements."

"Indeed? She is a medium?"

"Something of the kind, sir."

"You see—I do *like* the house. It is charming. And the price suits my pocket." Mr. Teazel nodded sympathetically. Marcus did not mention his circumstances, but they had found their way sufficiently often into the popular press. Alimony payments constituted a colossal drain on his resources. His ex-wife, an ex-actress twenty years younger than himself, showed no signs of ever intending to remarry or reenter her former profession.

Marcus went on: "I like the house. The price is right. But—in view of my best-known programs—a ghost would certainly be expected. It would be humiliating to occupy the only unhaunted cottage in a town otherwise infested by spooks. It would not do."

"Then," said Mr. Teazel, "I have no hesitation in recommending the services of Mrs. Spearpoint. If that is the only problem, consider the deal clinched, Mr. Fantail!"

Mrs. Spearpoint occupied picturesque premises just beyond the venerable gray stone towers and arch of the Land Gate. Her shop was bow-windowed, bristling with colored raffia mats, gleaming with lusterware jugs, Indian silks, rustling with dried flowers; a large green and red parrot occupied a perch over a sign that said NOT FOR SALE. Mrs. Spearpoint, in contrast to her wares, was a pale, attenuated, soft, silvery, muted lady, in the borderland between middle-aged and elderly. But the beam of attention that she trained on Marcus Fantail was like a lighthouse ray; her awareness of him appeared to be total. And in her silences could be heard echoes of sounds otherwise impossibly faint and far away, like the pulsing of distant deeply buried underground waters.

"So you are in need of an entity, Mr. Fantail?" was what she said. "Can you tell me why?"

Very slightly embarrassed, he explained the social and professional nature of his need. It was soon evident to him that Mrs. Spearpoint never watched television, did not understand the ABC of his references, had never even heard of *A Phantom at the Fireside;* however, her lightning-swift, razor-sharp intelligence obviated the need for any complicated explanations. Marcus did, though, to his own surprise, find that he was giving her an account of why a man in his otherwise favorable financial position could not at this time afford one of the more expensive, ready-haunted mansions that stood so much higher in the town's hierarchy.

"Your wife, Gloria. I perfectly understand—and have you been parted for long?"

"For the last ten years. Ever—ever since my son, our son—ever since our son died."

He did not expand on that, and she did not inquire.

With a somewhat startling switch to rapid, businesslike efficiency, she began to lay before him the various choices with which he was presented, going into poltergeist, banshee, footsteps, psychic cold, elementals, howls, telekinesis, appearances, disappearances, supernatural flames—a whole catalog of paranormal phenomena.

"These can all be introduced at will?"

"Oh, my dear sir—" Mrs. Spearpoint kindly overlooked the note of skepticism in his tone. "You must understand that, to persons of perception, this whole planet is packed, is lined, is layered with such emanations. Imagine a suitcase completely filled with spiders' webs, crammed so that the lid will hardly shut. Remember the countless millennia that have passed, the infinity of spirits that have been liberated from their earthly envelopes. Where are they? All around us. And all that you request is for just *one* to be transferred— decanted, as it were, from one location to another."

In spite of himself, Marcus began to find her convincing.

"Put like that, it does sound simple," he admitted. "So, when—when can you do it? Ideally I should like to move in next month."

"No problem, my dear Mr. Fantail. No problem at all."

By what means Mrs. Spearpoint went about her business, Marcus was not informed, nor did he inquire. He preferred in fact not to know. The process of his departure from Hyperion TV, the business of closing his Marylebone flat, disposing of his assets, transporting his furniture, occupied all his energies, nowadays also much depleted by the disease of the aorta that had necessitated his early retirement.

He settled Mrs. Spearpoint's four-figure account without a murmur, being of the type that is impressed and convinced by any price if only it is high enough. And after all, he thought comfortably, I can always sue the old girl if nothing turns up.

Before leaving Marylebone he had an acrimonious conversation with Gloria, who had of course read about his early retirement in the daily press and telephoned him to make sure that her allowance would not lapse from its present level.

"How come you can afford to move to a fancy little dump like Crowbridge?" she inquired disagreeably. "I know about that place. Glenda Pilbeam lived there with her second husband."

"Don't worry, don't worry." He suppressed the words *you bloodsucking bitch*—his doctor had warned that any strong emotion such as anger would be very deleterious in his condition. He told her mildly that he expected the town's ambience would produce many ideas for future free-lance television work.

"Oh, I see," she said, sounding relieved, but then added spitefully, "How you can go on doing that kind of thing—how you can bear to make a living from all that revolting melodrama—when your own son—" Her voice ran up to a high pitch.

"That's enough, Gloria! That's quite enough! We won't go into that again. You had your hand in it too. If you had been—a different kind of mother—"

She began screaming. "You drove that boy to do what he did. If you had ever talked to Mark—"

"I can't stand this," he said, and put down the receiver.

Their rare conversations always ended in the same way.

Marcus unplugged the television, locked the door of the Marylebone flat for the last time, and made his way down to the hired limousine, which, since he could no longer drive, awaited him in the street.

The trip to Crowbridge took two and a half hours, through pleasant, hazy autumn weather, past gold and tawny oakwoods and gray, dismantled hopfields. Riding thus in unwonted freedom and relaxation, Marcus began, after all, to look forward to his retirement with its idle pleasures. I shall potter, he thought peacefully, I shall play records and tapes and talk to the neighbors. "If you had ever talked to Mark—" Gloria's furious words came back to him. How hideously unfair she was, he thought. In the old days, before Mark had become an alien, he and the boy had talked and talked for hours together, ranging over every possible topic. He remembered at random one of their discussions, on vacation, it must have been, when the boy still went on vacations with them, one rainy day on Skye. It had been about body language: the differing codes of manners to be found in different civilizations. Body language, he had said, was extremely important in TV programs. You could not hope to sell anything worldwide if it violated some powerful unspoken rule of conduct—"like showing the soles of your feet to somebody," he remembered Mark suggesting, that would be a shocking insult in some Oriental countries, and the conversation had ended in laughter as they envisaged other such gestures and the situations in which they might inadvertently occur. Do ghosts have body language? Are there codes of conduct for dwellers in the supernatural world?

Number Four, Bowstring Lane, looked peaceful and inviting when Marcus reached it: Late roses still bloomed in the tiny front garden; a light shone in the window. Mrs. Frint, the new housekeeper, would have turned on the heat and left a meal ready for him.

Unlocking the ancient oak door with his bright key, Marcus speculated rather cheerfully on what form Mrs. Spearpoint's psychic phenomenon might take. In the end he had left the choice to her. "Only I would rather it were not *noisy*," he stipulated. "That is unfair to the neighbors, and I personally don't care for loud bangs or howls or rappings."

And she had set down a note on her businesslike memo pad.

The cottage was warm, tranquil, friendly. Bypassing the lounge, doubtless, he thought, the site of any manifestation, Marcus went carefully up the short staircase to the master bedroom, pushed open the door, and switched on the light.

And saw before him on Lord Woolsack's green carpet, which he had purchased, the soles of two dirty bare feet, the toes turning outward into a terrible caricature of peace and relaxation. . . .

Gasping, with his hand to his heart, Marcus turned and fell headlong down the stairs.

"Poor gentleman, them steps must have been just too much for him, after his journey," said Mrs. Frint, who found him next morning, after she had dutifully summoned the police and local doctor. "Such a shame when he hadn't even moved in yet; and the house all so neat and tidy awaiting him—not a speck out of place!"

Number Four, Bowstring Lane, is again on the market.

Earrings

WHEN AUNT DIMSIE got married to Mr. Goss, I heard Ma say to Father that it was really a mercy, in some ways, that little Marjorie wasn't still alive, as, between them, Marjorie and Mr. Goss would have torn Aunt Dimsie in half.

"Marjorie wouldn't have been prepared to share her mother with a strange man," Ma said. "She was always such a demanding child, from the day she was born. Poor Dimsie—I don't know—perhaps it's better this way."

Pondering the interesting picture of Marjorie and Mr. Goss, each with an arm and a leg, I found myself in disagreement with Mother. I thought, If Marjorie were still alive, Aunt Dimsie wouldn't have married Mr. Goss. No way. Marjorie would have prevented it.

Marjorie *loathed* Mr. Goss.

And although I'd never been too wild about my cousin Marjorie, who kept pet doves in a dovecot, totally preferred birds to humans, and called me a stupid sop because I wasn't keen to go on ten-mile hikes through rain and brambles to look for a marsh warbler's nest, when it came to the question of Mr. Goss, I was heart and soul on Marjorie's side. Herbert Goss was big and massive and red-faced, baldish, with a ginger mustache, and had made his money, a whole lot of it, from inventing some nasty weapon, a kind of pocket machine gun that he sold to foreigners and terrorists so that they could kill each other with greater ease and speed.

Mr. Goss had retired from active business now (though he still derived a big income from his gun) so that he'd have all the time in the world to shout at Aunt Dimsie and bully her.

"I do pity her, poor woman, I must say," said Father. "She'd certainly have had an easier life being trampled underfoot by Marjorie."

Aunt Dimsie's first husband, Father's brother, Christy, had been killed five years ago in an air crash when Marjorie was nine. She'd have been fourteen the week of the wedding.

There was a tentative suggestion that I should be bridesmaid in Marjorie's place. I think it was Mr. Goss's idea. Ma thought it in shockingly poor taste.

"So soon after the tragedy—disgraceful! What about poor Dimsie's feelings?"

"Well, he still wants the big slap-up wedding with all the trimmings," said Father.

"I expect it's because they had the bridesmaid's dress all ready," I said. "Those blue and white stripes. Marjorie said she wouldn't be seen dead in them. Anyway I shan't accept. I don't want to walk along the aisle behind Mr. Goss. He's just like a big shark—teeth and all."

So, in the end, they managed without a bridesmaid.

* * *

We went to the wedding of course.

It was a *terrible* day. Rain from daybreak on, not just ordinary rain but real hard torrents of it, bucketing down. All through the wedding service you could hear it drumming and thundering on the church roof (and finding its way through, here and there—Tench Underhill church was built in 1100 and is in urgent need of repair; you could hear squeaks and moans from the congregation every once in a while as a big drop hit somebody's bald pate or feather hat). The inside of the church was as dim and misty as a bathroom full of steam; you could hardly see up the aisle. After the signing ceremony in the vestry there was no question of photographs at the church door—everybody simply made a bolt for their waiting cars.

"I really think I must need a holiday," muttered Ma when we were in our Renault driving glumly through the downpour. "It was so dark in the church—and stuffy—that several times I felt as if I might pass out. Once or twice, believe it or not, I could have sworn that I saw Marjorie standing behind Dimsie. In that blue and white dress."

"She'd never have worn it," I said. "She said it looked like a cleaning rag."

I didn't add that I thought I had seen Marjorie too. Holding a bouquet of gentians and freesias, scowling horribly at Mr. Goss.

The reception was held, not at Aunt Dimsie's little house, which was to be sold, but at Pine Hill, Mr. Goss's great place. It was large enough to house a trade-union conference, all polished, yellow-wood floors and square banister rails and massive newel posts and suits of false-looking armor, and stained-glass windows in every room, including the bathrooms. The wedding breakfast was served in a barnlike room with a minstrel gallery and two grand pianos, one at each end.

There was a great deal of jollity and a great many of Mr. Goss's friends, who were either built like him, with big square business faces and thinning streaks of hair draped carefully over the tops of their heads, or they were small and dark and ugly with unpronounceable names. I began to feel desperately sorry for Aunt Dimsie; and all the champagne in the world couldn't stop Ma from looking more and more depressed.

She and I went to help Aunt Dimsie change into her powder-blue going-away suit, in a bedroom the size of an airport runway with massive stone balconies outside the windows and a view of rain-drenched lawns and rhododendrons beyond, stretching away into the misty distance.

"It seems so cold in this house," said Aunt Dimsie, shivering.

"Well, of course you are bound to catch the wind here, in winter, up on this hilltop," agreed Ma. "But I'm sure Mr. Goss can afford the very best kind of central heating. Here, just turn around while I button you at the back."

"Oh, Edna—did I do right? Tell me I did! I d-do so miss d-darling Christy—and poor little M-Marjorie—and Linnet Cottage—"

"Of course you did right," said Ma in the sort of scolding voice she puts on when she really isn't so certain about something. "Herbert can give you a wonderful time. Now you need a bit of makeup—you're far too pale—"

"I keep thinking about Marjorie. Do you know— Herbert did such a kind thing—he moved all Marjorie's nesting boxes from Linnet into the shrubbery here. Wasn't that sweet of him?"

"It was indeed," Ma said rather drily.

"He knew how much I'd be missing Marjorie. I think, n-now she's gone," said Aunt Dimsie in a faltering voice, "Herbert appreciates her qualities more."

"I'm sure he does, my dear." Mother did not allude to the terrible things Marjorie used to say about Mr. Goss, or his retaliations. "There—now you look very nice. Which earrings are you going to wear?"

"Oh—that reminds me." Aunt Dimsie turned and rummaged in her little going-away case. "Here, Lucy darling—these are for you. Marjorie was—she was to have worn them as bridesmaid—her godmother, my friend Geraldine, left them to her. Now I want you to have them."

"Oh, Aunt Dimsie—thank you!" I stammered. "They—they are beautiful."

"Geraldine brought them back from one of her field trips," said Aunt Dimsie. "They were made by the Skahoe Indians."

They were long, dangling complicated spirals—two spirals, one inside the other—made of delicate silver with tiny green stones.

Geraldine Stannery had been Aunt Dimsie's greatest friend. They had met at college and kept up ever since, seeing each other every couple of weeks, corresponding when apart. Geraldine was an anthropologist and spent years of her life studying the habits of primitive tribes. In the end she just didn't return from one of her long field trips. (Just as well, maybe, for she and Mr. Goss didn't get on at all.) It was odd that she and Dimsie should have been so devoted, when you think how different they were.

"There was another thing that went with the earrings," said Dimsie. "Here it is."

She handed me a circlet about five inches in circumference, made of thin, stiff bark. Across it, crisscross, was woven a network of fine grasses.

"It's a dream catcher," said Dimsie. "You put it by your bed, Geraldine told me, and it is supposed to drive away bad dreams. And bring pleasant ones."

She smiled at me wanly. I wondered if she had been using it herself. If so, she wasn't a particularly good advertisement for its magic power.

"DIM—SIE!" yelled Herbert Goss. "Aren't you ready *yet*? Get a move on! We're going to miss that plane!"

We heard him come thumping up the wide pine stairs and Aunt Dimsie quivered a little, then gulped and hugged Ma.

"Good-bye, darling Edna—thanks for everything. Good-bye, Lucy dear—keep an eye on Marjorie's doves in their nesting boxes, will you, if you have time—?"

She pulled herself away from us and made for the door, just as Herbert came bursting in.

"Ready at last? So I should hope! Come on, then!"

He whisked her around and almost shoved her down the stairs.

Mother and I followed more slowly, Ma turning first to give a slow, puzzled stare around the big shiny room with its four-poster bed, glass-topped furnishings, velvet curtains, and furry white carpet.

There was a white quilted stool in front of the dressing table with its huge triple mirror. I wondered if Ma had thought she saw what *I* thought I had seen: the reflection, in the glass, of my cousin Marjorie, squatting on the padded stool, her arms around her knees, directing a silent, malignant glare toward Herbert Goss.

But I said nothing to my mother, nor she to me.

By the time we loitered downstairs, the good-byes had already been said, and the married pair, in their Rolls, were being driven away through the deluge.

We didn't linger on with the rest of the invitees, drinking more champagne, but made for our own small, messy car.

"Thank the lord that's over," said my father. "Now I can put my best suit back into mothballs for another nine years."

"I do hope to goodness Dimsie doesn't regret it," Ma was muttering as the windscreen wipers scraped and squeaked.

"Well, at least she's not our worry anymore," said Father rather heartlessly.

When we got back to the house, Mother made me hand over Aunt Dimsie's earrings in their little silk-lined box. "Far too good for you just yet. Perhaps when you are a year or two older . . ."

In a way I wasn't sorry. Although they were very beautiful, there was something snaky and hypnotic about the concentric spirals; they almost seemed to move and squirm by themselves as they lay in their silk nest. And they were so long that I thought they might be a nuisance, even dangerous; they would dangle and swing and catch in my hair or collar.

"Besides, you haven't had your ears pierced yet," Ma went on.

I resolved to have this remedied without delay— most of my friends already had—and also to switch to a shorter hairstyle; both of which programs I carried out. Yet I never got around to reminding Mother about the earrings; although it wasn't that I didn't think of them, from time to time, lying there quietly in her top left-hand drawer.

Once in a while I'd go and look at them, when Ma and Father were out and I was alone in the house.

There they lay.

In the course of time Aunt Dimsie and (as we were now instructed to call him) Uncle Herbert came home to Pine Hill. His wedding gift to her had been a trip around the world, so by the time they got back they were tanned and weathered, and full of stories about disastrous flights and magnificent beaches. Herbert was several inches fatter, whereas Dimsie seemed to have shrunk—she looked as thin, brown, and gnarled as one of those dwarf Japanese trees people plant in rock gardens. Ma had to suppress a yelp of horror at the sight of her.

Herbert, however, was thoroughly pleased with himself.

"Just the right time of year to come home." (It was April.) "Had a first-class garden firm come last autumn and put in thousands of bulbs at Pine Hill. Really paid off. It's a grand sight now—good as a bulb catalog."

I knew that, because I'd walked across the valley now and then to check on Marjorie's nesting boxes. Acres of huge double daffodils the color of mustard sauce, masses of hyacinths, bigger than chimney pots, in violent pinks, blues, and mauves; hideous little miniature double-pink cherry trees like marshmallow explosions.

"Pine Hill really is a sight," Herbert said again complacently. "You must all come over to lunch on Saturday and enjoy it."

Father said, terribly sorry, he had a complicated case on at court, needed a lot of reading, couldn't make it. Which left Ma and me to go dismally on our own. Dimsie, at parting, had given us such fervent, beseeching hugs that we couldn't deny her.

"Please come! It's so wonderful to see you again," she said, looking at us piteously out of eyes that seemed disproportionately large, sunk in their shadowy netted pits in her drawn face. "Do you wear Marjorie's earrings sometimes?" she asked me.

"Er—well—I keep them for special occasions," I mumbled.

"Do wear them on Saturday, dearie. I'd love to see them being used. They'll remind me of Marjorie and my darling Geraldine."

"Darling Geraldine!" scoffed Herbert, overhearing. There was a disagreeable sneer on his face. "Now *there* was an old witch if ever there was one. I don't suppose anybody cried buckets at her end, when she was eaten by the Yamahazbecs (or whoever finished her off)—except poor old Dimsie here, who, let's face it, hasn't much judgment when it comes to picking friends. Geraldine! She's no loss to the world." And he went on in this vein for several minutes more.

Poor old Dimsie cringed, gave us a hunted, harassed look, and allowed herself to be shoveled into the car.

That was enough to make Ma get out the earrings later and say to me, "You'd better wear these on Saturday, Lucy. But mind you take good care of them. . . ."

"Of course I'll wear them," I said. "I'd planned to."

"What's this?" Ma fished out a flat tissue-paper package from under the earring box and eyed it in bafflement. "Oh, I know, it's that other thing Dimsie gave you. I forget now what she said."

"A dream catcher. Drives away bad dreams and brings good ones. I wonder how you are supposed to use it?"

Mother, abandoning interest, went away to telephone her sister Sylvia and tell her about the hideous effect that marriage to Herbert had had on poor Aunt Dimsie; I took the earrings and the dream catcher off to my bedroom. I studied the earrings in their box— touched them a little to see them shimmer—but decided not to put them on at present. Not just yet. The dream catcher I hung on a thread over the head of my bed. No reason why that shouldn't be put to use. Not that, in the general way, I do have bad dreams; on the whole I greatly enjoy my dreams, which are full of unexpected events and interesting people. In the old days I used to relate them to Marjorie, who, poor thing, could never come up with anything half as entertaining. Hers were mostly about birds. And she found mine terribly tedious.

But that night I had a real monster of a dream.

I was falling down a dark, soft precipice. There was nothing to grab on to except friable, black, crumbly stuff that came away in my fingers as I touched it. And there was nothing to breathe, except the same black horrible stuff, which poured into eyes, mouth, nose, and lungs, blinding, choking, and suffocating. I was falling, sliding, choking, *done for.* I was going to die. And I *did* die. The dream did not end in a scream, hurling myself out of bed and into wakefulness, as my infrequent nightmares tend to, but just moved on into sleep, so that next morning I had it clear, whole, and dreadful in my mind the very instant I woke.

Now, *now* I knew just how Marjorie had felt as she died.

We had known the bare facts of the story before of course. She had taken refuge from a thunderstorm (it was assumed) in a farmer's haybarn about five miles from home when she was off on one of her bird-watching hikes. Climbed on top of the hay, which was last year's, old and moldy, accidentally slipped down in the deep crevice between hay and barn wall, and somehow asphyxiated from the fumes of the decomposing stuff. Not found until several days later. A dreadful, dreadful tragedy, as everyone agreed, but at least the poor girl can't have suffered much: Her lungs were full of hay, she was almost certainly unconscious and never realized what was happening to her. That was what people said.

But now I knew better.

The morning was gray, overcast, and sultry, not like a spring day, more like one in August when a storm's due. I felt not unwell but just wretched, the way one does after getting a horrible piece of bad news, the knowledge of which will always be there from now on, inescapable, coloring everything else.

When Mother said, "What are you going to wear?" I almost growled at her, "Oh, what does it matter what we wear?"

In the end I chose a green pleated silky dress Aunt Dimsie had given me last year, one of a pair she brought back from a Venetian vacation with Geraldine Stannery. She had given Marjorie the other dress. Green suited Marjorie's dark coloring. I don't care for the color and hardly ever wore the dress.

"A very tactful thought," said Ma approvingly. "And it will go with the earrings."

I left putting them on till the last minute before we started. They were surprisingly heavy. I could feel them swing and dangle and twirl as I walked to the car; I had the rather crazy impression that two tiny people were hanging from my earlobes.

There was another very odd thing that I soon noticed about them, and so did Ma.

"What's that whistling noise?" she said, getting out her car keys.

"It's these earrings. They seem to catch the wind. Like Chinese windbells."

"But there isn't any wind to speak of."

It was a still, heavy, hushed day, more like midsummer than April.

"Why should *you* have the earrings?" whispered Marjorie's voice in my ear as we drove along. "They weren't bought for you. You've no right to them. And I never liked you anyway."

The leaves on the trees were still tiny, pale green, and glistening—until we drove up the approach to Pine Hill, where huge rhododendrons with dark foliage and flowers the color of blood rose up like ramparts on either side of the drive. Then, beyond them, we saw the massed mustard yellow and washing-powder white of the daffs and narcissi stretching away in lavish carpets.

And all along the drive Marjorie's earrings were whispering and nagging in my ears.

"He did it, he did it, Herbert did it! He gave me a packet of drugged nuts; he knew I couldn't resist macadamia nuts. And when I got drowsy, he took me to that place and pushed me down. He did it. Herbert killed me."

"Do stop whistling under your breath, Lucy," Ma said. "I can't stand it as I drive."

"I'm not whistling. . . ."

Herbert was there to meet us at the portico, all jollity and hostliness.

"Before you come indoors, walk around the side and see the daffs on the south lawn," he boomed. "If you think these are spectacular, just you wait!"

After one rather startled glance at me, he kept his eyes firmly on Ma, but Aunt Dimsie, behind him, said, "Oh, how nice you look, Lucy dear, in that dress. And I am so pleased to see you wearing the earrings."

I wondered if Dimsie could hear them as well as see them. Their whisper was now a hiss, loud as the sound of wind through dry rushes: "Herbert, Herbert, Herbert, Herbert, killed me, killed me, killed me, killed me."

"I think I'm going to have to take them off," I mumbled unhappily. "I'm not used to wearing such heavy ones."

"Just wait, dear, till we are in the house. Then you can come to my room."

The room, I remembered, where I had seen Marjorie reflected in the triple mirror. And yet she had never set foot inside Pine Hill.

As I thought that, I saw Marjorie, herself, wearing a green dress the twin of mine, move out of a door in a wall enclosing a vegetable garden and walk along, just behind Uncle Herbert.

We were following a neatly tended gravel path between the great yellow plastic plains of daffodils. It led toward a shrubbery. More rhododendrons grew there, scarlet, flame colored, and salmon pink.

I saw Ma give Marjorie a quick, puzzled glance and

then look hastily back at me. Aunt Dimsie, apparently unaware of anything unusual, was talking in a breathless, feverish twitter, about the flowers they had seen on their travels.

"Put a sock in it, can't you, woman?" Herbert called back impatiently. "Let the guests get a word in edgeways."

His mood seemed suddenly to have shot downhill.

At the entrance to the shrubbery he turned and said, "I'm bringing you this way because Dimsie is always going on about how I didn't love her precious little Marjie. I'm taking you to show you what I did in memory of her precious little Marjie. And then you can decide for yourselves if I am such a mean old stick as Dimsie is always making out."

"I never, never said, Herbert—" Dimsie began timidly, but he had turned and was striding on. He appeared not to see Marjorie, in her green dress, silently keeping pace just behind him. Nor, it appeared, did Aunt Dimsie see her daughter, though once she did put out her hand in a puzzled, beseeching gesture.

We came to a clearing in the shrubbery. It was like a little courtyard, paved with cobbles, walled with yew hedges. Marjorie's nesting boxes for the doves had been set up all around it. I had been here once or twice in the course of the spring and knew that the doves were nesting well, seemingly not bothered by their change of habitat. Flocks of the white creatures—more, I thought, than ever before—were fluttering about, bustling back and forth, taking off on excursions over the rhododendrons, returning again to their nests.

But there was something new since I had been here before: In the center a gray marble statue of Marjorie, standing, hands on hips in a characteristic posture, looking up at her bird boxes.

"There! Had that done as a surprise for Dimsie, while we were away! That chap Fenimoore who does them from photos. Remarkable likeness, ain't it?" demanded Herbert, recovering his joviality.

It *was* a good likeness. It cruelly rendered all Marjorie's plainness—her glasses, big nose, bad skin, hair scraped ungracefully back, thickset body, shapeless legs. She was wearing a school tunic, most hideous and unbecoming of garments, wrinkled socks, and sneakers with the laces coming undone.

"*Marvelous* likeness, ain't it?" repeated Herbert fondly.

By now the earrings in my ears were fairly yelling: "He killed me, he killed me, *Herbert killed me*!" I saw Ma turn and throw me a startled look. Beyond her I saw Marjorie, in the green dress, walk between the doves' boxes into the middle of the circle and give the statue an angry push. It fell over, as if it were made of *papier-mâché*, with a loud crash and a cloud of dust.

Herbert spun around, his mouth wide open.

Marjorie now stood where the statue had been, in precisely the same attitude, hands on hips. Then she clapped her hands together sharply, once.

All the doves rose up together in a mob—a white, flapping, whirling, raucous mob—they sounded more like a swarm of rowdy rooks than a decorous flock of demure white doves. Next, with one accord, they swooped down upon Herbert.

In a moment he was covered all over with the white things—face, head, eyes, arms, hands. He looked like a big macaroon that has been rolled on coconut flakes.

He began to scream. "Get them off! Get them bloody off! Help me! Help me get rid of the buggers!" His words were muffled by feathers, by birds. Then he rushed away, beating with his arms, down one of the paths that led away from the clearing. The doves went along, too, perching, swooping, and pecking. In a moment they were out of sight. We heard him screaming in the distance.

Dimsie fainted, dead away, on the cobbles.

"Help me get her back to the house," said Ma, white-lipped. Her teeth were chattering, and so were mine.

I carried Dimsie's feet, Ma her shoulders. A gardener met us halfway and offered to take Dimsie, but Ma told him he'd better go and help Mr. Goss, who was having trouble with the birds. Off he went, and we, once indoors, assisted by Mrs. Wade, the housekeeper, gave Dimsie brandy, and held ammonia under her nose.

After a while she came to, looked at us in a puzzled way, and said, "I saw Marjorie. In the shrubbery. I saw my daughter Marjorie."

"Just take it easy now, dear," said Mrs. Wade, slipping in another spoonful of brandy.

By and by the gardener came in, white as paint. "What is it, Wilkins?" snapped the housekeeper. "You shouldn't be in here."

"I can't find Mr. Goss," said the man hoarsely. "All I could find—well, mum, I think you'd best come and see."

Mother and I went with him, both of us walking slowly on legs that trembled a good deal. And he showed us, at the far end of the shrubbery, a patch of blood on the path. The blood had soaked into the gravel, and the patch was the size and shape of a man.

That was all there was to see—blood, and a few shreds of leather and tweed. And a belt buckle.

No further trace of Herbert ever came to light.

Later on I gave the earrings back to Aunt Dimsie. They were beautiful, but too heavy for me, I said.

An L-Shaped Grave

THE ARTIST'S NAME was Luna Knox, and the show of sculptures was billed simply as "self-portraits." And it was being held in a most inaccessible part of town, thought Maurice Hart, the art critic, staring irritably out the dirty train window at monotonous rows of suburban roofs slipping past with their dank December gardens and gray, leafless trees. One of the houses, to Hart's mild wonder, had a moose head attached to its wall, the kind of trophy usually to be found indoors, in hunting lodges and baronial halls. How very singular to set it up out of doors, he mused; but then it occurred to him that a moose is, after all, an outdoor animal, accustomed to life in the wild; the oddity, really, is in fetching the beast inside four walls. Another house, a short distance farther on, had a sign: "Mathematics Lessons: call 03339-9966." How many rail passengers would be in need of math lessons and would trouble to call that number, activated by a sign seen so briefly through grimed, rain-streaked glass? But many people, he supposed, traveled to and from their work along this piece of track ten times every week; to them the moose, the math lessons, must be an accustomed part of their daily ritual.

Gresham Common, Lordsfield, Crittleworth . . . and now the track, taking a wide curve on its raised embankment, circled back toward the river, into a region that must once have been tidal marshes, but now, long reclaimed, held docks and warehouses. Ancient rusty derricks loomed among grass-grown, littered trackways and half-derelict buildings. The district was, in fact, being transformed yet again, as waterborne trade took to the air and shipping sadly declined. Now the spacious, lofty warehouses were being converted into art galleries and artists' studios, rents were soaring, and ships' chandler's stores were experiencing a new lease on life as expensive boutiques offering frivolous, impractical luxuries and exotic trifles in place of their former sternly utilitarian wares. The principal virtue of the new goods offered for sale was that they could be billed as ethnic; the actual source of origin was of little importance so long as it was somewhere overseas.

Hopford Dock: Maurice Hart stood up, buttoned his raincoat, and with considerable reluctance left the warmth of the stuffy carriage. Hopford Dock station was no more than a halt, a one-walled shelter with steps leading down to the unexplored wilderness below.

Dusk had already begun to fall, though it was hardly past three on a disagreeable afternoon. Hart wished that he could have come by car, but an unfortunate drunk-driving episode had rendered him subject to a three-month ban; hoisting his shoulders, turning up his collar, he strode out along a roadway bordered on both sides by the bulky rectangular shapes of storehouses or factories—how to find street names in this derelict area? Impatiently he hurried on, occasionally consulting the small conventional map printed on his card of invitation, realizing with added annoyance that he might as well have quitted the train at the previous stop and saved himself a walk: There was the house with the moose, getting sleeker with wet all the time. At last he came to a street sign—Rope Walk—and was able to orient himself. He took a left turn, then a right, and suddenly found himself among people and lights; brilliant shop windows were filled with glistening swaths of fabric, dazzling pyramids of crystal, colors that appeared to seethe and bubble as elixirs might in the alchemist's crucible. The people in this thorough-fare, which had apparently been closed to wheeled traf-fic, were all young, their clothes ran to the wildest ex-treme of contemporary taste. They wore huge hats, high-heeled boots, shawls, turbans, dhotis, breeches, serapes, bustles, cloaks whose gaudy hues throbbed like the music of tom-toms in the dusk and drizzle.

"Is this Watergate Lane?" Hart asked. "I'm looking for the Crane Galleries."

"Right there, man! Right ahead of you!"—and in the same moment he saw it, a wrought-iron sign that, in eccentric lettering, spelled out the word CRANE up the side of a narrow, lofty building.

Hart showed his card, after passing through a mas-sive glass door that opened to him automatically, then signed his name in a book that lay on a large metal barrel. Behind the barrel was what appeared to be an organ constructed out of monumental steam pipes and valves left over from some discarded piece of machin-ery. He noted this with slight disapproval, and pro-ceeded through an inner door into the gallery itself, where he was immediately handed a large glass of red wine.

So far, so good, he thought drily, sipping the beverage (which, he must admit, was not bad at all, powerful and with an excellent bouquet).

The building was full of people, yet so very large that the crowd was of little more importance than acorns on the floor of a forest. The place had been a warehouse once, the ceiling, almost out of sight, supported by mighty cast-iron pillars with filigree ornamentation and Corinthian capitals. These, and the walls and ceiling, had been painted stark, arctic white; and the floor, composed of some hard, resonant wood, was polished to an arctic glitter. Yet the enormous bare room was not cold. Nor was it noisy; the voices of the guests became muted, soft, and awestruck as they strolled and wandered with glasses in their hands. Tiny sparks of red light, reflected from the wine in the glasses, moved and flickered on the white walls. The light came from lusters which were hung, rather frivolously and eccentrically, on twenty to thirty pairs of deer's antlers, which had been suspended on white ropes high above the guests and the exhibits.

These were what Hart had come to see, and what he noticed last. Yet once he had taken them in, he ceased to observe anything else at all: the white walls; the large mirrors on the walls; the monumental white pillars; the black, lumpy shapes of the crowding people; the red-flashing reflections—all sank through his mind like salt dissolving in water.

The pieces, of which there might have been twenty or so, were from six to seven feet high, and they had been constructed, Hart read, consulting his card, from epoxy, cloth, and bronze or aluminum powder. The cloth had been somehow impregnated with the glue and powdered metal, then coaxed into folds and drapings, then left to harden. The material, thus stiffened, suggested the outline of a figure inside; but the figure was lacking. Here was a cloaked, hooded massive woman: but the space below the browband of the hood was vacant, merely a dark hole; no eyes looked out. Folds of gray cloth conveyed the shape of a breast, a nipple; but a slit down the side of the robe, from armpit to ankle, showed dark emptiness inside. Draperies blown back on a ship's figurehead outlined a graceful torso, but, stepping behind this figure, Hart found it to be concave at the rear, no more than a hollow shell.

"Hey, Hart, me old son!" said a voice in his ear. "What do you think of them?" and, turning, he saw the face of a fellow critic, a man called McDougal, who wrote a weekly column for the *Sunday Landmark.* "What d'you think?" McDougal repeated. "Not bad? You gave the girl a real pasting last time, didn't you? Heroic groups, wasn't it, all made out of hemp?"

"These are better. Clever," admitted Hart, a shade reluctantly. "Frozen motion. Not a new idea, but she's done it capably, I must admit—"

"But—?"

"But—don't you feel there is an element missing? And I *don't* mean just the bodies inside," he added defensively.

"What, then?"

"What's between dark and light, between moonbeams and sunshine?"

"Much too philosophical for me, old boy," said McDougal, clapping him on the shoulder. "And you'd

better not speak too loud. The lady herself is somewhere about; I saw her just now."

"Oh? I've never met her. What sort of age?"

"Hard to say. She might reasonably feel she has a
grudge against you—after what you wrote last time.
I've heard she can be quite tough with fellows who get
on her bad side. You'd better give her a nice boost this
time."

"Can't promise," snapped Hart. "I can only say
what I think, can't I? I came to her flaming show, didn't
I? And a nice trip I had of it, all the way out to this
godforsaken spot. Anyway, I don't wholly dislike them.
They're better than the last lot at least. There is something a bit mysterious about them—"

Then he realized that McDougal had stepped away
and that he was addressing instead the back of some
female in a black dress who stood with her head turned
away from him. Her hair was black, too, and there must
have been yards of it, enough to reach to her ankles if it
had been let down, but it was coiled and plaited into an
intricate structure, a kind of coronet on the back of her
head, and two long, twisted locks fell on either side of
her face. The face, he now discovered, was dimly dis-
cernible to him in the mirror on the wall beyond her;
he could see sparks of light reflected in her eyes and
some kind of a sparkling crescent pinned on the crown
of hair. She began to speak without turning around and,
from her tone of mockery, he supposed that her words
were intended for him.

"So you actually came all the way out to this
godforsaken spot, Mr. Hart, did you? And you like these
better than the last lot? I wonder by which God do you
suppose this spot *was* forsaken, Mr. Hart? By Apollo,
perhaps? Or by Wotan? Or Allah? Or Jehovah?"

"Oh, just a manner of speech, you know," he said uncomfortably. "Are you—am I right in guessing that you are Luna Knox? The pieces are quite original. You heard me say there was something mysterious about them—"

"Yes, and something missing as well. I wonder what that something can be, Mr. Hart?"

Still she went on admonishing him in the glass, with her back turned, and he exclaimed angrily, "I wish you would turn around and talk to me properly! This is an idiotic way to hold a conversation."

"You wish that I would speak to you directly? Oh, but that wouldn't do, Mr. Hart, that wouldn't do at all. No, I fear you must look for me in the mirror. I very much fear that if you looked at me directly, something unfortunate might happen. People have been blinded who stared into the naked light of the sun, Mr. Hart. Perhaps that is why I leave something out of my works. No, I am afraid you might find the sight of my face much too disturbing—"

With a furious exclamation he laid his hand on her shoulder and pulled her around to face him.

Heads turned in the crowd at the clatter of broken glass and a series of cataclysmic screams. Startled guests jumped aside as Hart, flailing with his fists, staggering, lurching, made his way to the lobby and out through the automatic doors, which mockingly parted to permit his exit.

All the way along the street his shrieks continued: "My head, my head, oh God, my head!"

When he was picked up, at the end of Watergate Lane, he was clasping his temples with both hands, as if to contain intolerable agony. And he had grown a full-size pair of elk's antlers; it was thought his death must have been caused by a brain hemorrhage.

The antlers were so large, indeed, that it was necessary to dig an L-shaped grave in order to accommodate both him and them.

Something

WHEN THE THING HAPPENED for the first time, I was digging up wild lilies to plant in my own little garden. Digging up wild lilies. A happy task. They are dark orange and grow down by the narrow shallow brook that freezes solid in winter. On that day it was babbling and murmuring placidly, and I sang a song, which I made up as I went along, to keep company with its murmur. "Wild lilies I find, wild lilies I bring, wild lilies, wild lilies, to flower in the spring." Overhead the alder trees arched, and water birds, becoming used to my harmless presence, called their short, gargling answers. Once or twice a kingfisher flashed. There were trout in the water, but only tiny ones; I could feel them brush against my bare legs every now and then as I waded knee-deep along the course of the brook, which made an easier route than the tangled banks.

At the end of a whole afternoon spent in this manner my mind felt bare, washed clean, like the stones in the brook.

And then—suddenly: fear. Where did it come from?

I had no means of knowing. *Menace.* Cold fear was all around me—in the dark arch of the trees, the tunnel they made (into which the stream vanished), the sharp croak of birds, the icy grip of the water on my calves, the gritty scour of the mud on my grimed and scraped hands. But, most of all, in my own mind, as if, down at the back of it, stood something hidden, watchful, *waiting.* In another minute I would see it and know what it was. In another minute I would go mad from terror.

Frenzied with haste to be away from there, I scrambled up the bank, snatching my trowel and the wooden bucket in which I had been putting my lily roots—dropping half of them; panic-stricken, never looking back, I thrust and battered a track through alders and brambles, tearing my shirt, scratching my arms and face. Mother would be furious, but I never gave that a thought. All my need was to get home—home—home to Grandfather's comforting presence.

Barefoot I ran over the plowed field, stubbing my toes on flints, reckless of sharp stubble ends and dry thistles with their lancing spines. Tonight I would need to spend hours squeezing them out, painfully one by one. Tonight was not now. Now if I did not find Grandfather, I would die of fear.

Luckily he was always to be found in the same place: placid on a backless chair with his dog, Flag, beside him, outside the smithy where my uncles Josef and Willi clanked on the anvil and roared on the bellows. A great gray cart horse waited patiently, one hoof tipped forward. A cone of fire burned bright in the dim forge, and there was Uncle Josef in his black leather apron, holding the gold and blazing shoe in his long tongs. For once I didn't wait and watch. I ran and clung tight to

Grandfather. He felt frail and bony, and smelled, as always, of straw and old man's odor, and sweet tobacco.

"Grandfather—Grandfather—" I gulped.

Holding me in thin, strong old hands, he looked at me long and shrewdly with his faded, shrunken eyes.

"So it's happened, has it?"

"Yes. Yes. It has. But what *is* it, Grandfather? *What* has happened?"

"Easy. Easy!" He soothed me with his voice as if I had been a panicky foal. "It was bound to come. It always does. Your father—your brothers—now you. All our family. It always happens, sooner or later."

"But what? But what?"

A terrific fusillade of clangs came from the forge. Uncle Josef had the shoe back on the anvil and was reshaping it with powerful blows of his hammer. A fan of sparks rained out, making the cart horse stamp and whinny.

"Come along," said my grandfather. "We'll walk to the church." He put his hand on my shoulder to hoist himself into a walking position, then kept it there, for balance. He was very stooped, and walked with a limp; still, for his years, he was as strong as an old root.

We went slowly along the village street. Marigolds blazed, nasturtiums climbed up the sides of the ancient timbered houses. Apples on the trees were almost ripe. The sky, though cloudless and blue as a gentian, was covered with a light haze; in the mornings and evenings now, mist lay thick in the valley. It was September.

"Winter is coming," said my grandfather.

"Yes, Grandfather."

"Winter is a kind of night," he said. "For months we are prisoners here in the village. As, at night, we are shut in our homes. The next village is a world's end away."

It was true. Our village lies in a deep valley. Often in winter the roads are blocked with snow for weeks, sometimes for months. Up to now I had never minded this. It was good fun, being closed away from the world. We had huge stacks of firewood—cellars full of wine and flour. The cows and sheep were stabled safely. We had dried fruits, stored apples, fiddles, music, jokes, and a few books. We had each other. What more did we need? Up to now I had loved the winter. But at this moment I shivered as I pictured miles of gale-scoured hills, the snow sent by wind into long, curving drifts, with never a human footprint. Darkness over the mountains for thirteen hours, from sunset to sunrise.

"Night is a kind of death," said my grandfather. And then: "You know that I have bad dreams."

Indeed I *did*. His yells when he woke from one of those legendary dreams were terrible to hear; they almost made the blood run backward in your veins. Yet he would never tell us what the dream had been about; he would sit (once he was awake), white, panting, shaking, gasping, by his bed; sometimes he might have hurled himself right out of his cot, an arm's length away from it and, next day, would be covered in black bruises, and his eyes sunken into deep, gray hollows.

But what the dream was about he would never reveal. Except perhaps to his old dog, Flag, who had trotted behind us, never more than a yard away, along the village street. During the hours of daylight Flag never left my grandfather; and at night, when all the dogs were left downstairs to guard the house and the livestock in the back stable, Flag invariably seemed to know beforehand if my grandfather was going to have one of his bad dreams; in his own sleep he would whine and snuffle; or, often, he would be awake and trembling at the foot of the stairs all night long. And next day Grandfather, bruised, breathless, staring, and shaky as he was, would be especially kind to Flag and feed him crusts of brown bread dipped in schnapps and honey.

"You know that I have bad dreams," repeated my grandfather.

"Yes, Opar; I know that. We all know it. And we are very sorry for you."

It seemed unfair that such a good, kind man should have such dreadful dreams. All his harmless life had been lived in the village. All his deeds were known. Never had he raised his hand unjustly or spoken in malice against another man. Why should *he* have to suffer such an affliction?

We came to the small graveyard where, under wooden crosses and between browsing goats, lay his father, my great-grandfather, and *his* father, and all my great-uncles and great-great-uncles and so on, back into the past for hundreds of years.

My grandfather looked gravely and gently at the crosses as if they were old companions from a whole series of hard-fought battles.

"What do we know about being dead?" he said. "Nothing, really."

Old Flag lay down, panting, and Grandfather sat on the low wall. Then he gave me a severe look.

"You don't have any friends," he said.

"Well—how can I, Grandfather? There just isn't anybody my age. Everybody else in the village is either too old for me or too young."

He sighed. "Yes; that's true enough. But tell me now—and tell the truth—when you are by yourself, as you were this afternoon, do you have a made-up friend in your own mind, a dream friend, a wish friend, who comes and talks to you?"

I blushed.

"Yes—well—just sometimes—not very often—"

"One friend—or several?"

"One."

My imaginary friend, Milo, who kept me company sometimes, and laughed at my jokes, and praised me if I had done well in my lessons with Father Tomas.

"Send that being away!" said my grandfather strongly. "Send him away and never, never let him come again. Such friends are—can be—very, very dangerous!"

"But, Grandfather, why?"

"Have you ever thought about your brothers?" he said. "Have you ever wondered why Anatol went to be a monk, why Peter joined the army?"

My brothers were many years older than myself. To be honest, I had never wondered about them at all.

"To be like my father—like Uncle Christian?" I suggested.

Grandfather carefully filled his pipe with strong, sweet-smelling tobacco.

"To be like them—yes," he said between puffs as he lit it. "But also for the same reason. No doubt your brother Peter will be killed, as your father was. No doubt Anatol will be lost to us, as your uncle Christian was. But *this* is the reason why they went: A soldier is never alone, for he is always surrounded by other soldiers. Likewise, a monk is never alone, for he is with other monks."

"And in the company of God too?" I suggested.

"Humph! That depends on the man, I'd say."

Grandfather stared, frowning, at the small, ancient church, as if he did not quite know where to fit it into the picture that was forming in his mind. Then he went on. "The men of our family do not dare to be alone."

"I don't understand—"

"Something happened, once, to our ancestor—"

"Which ancestor?"

"Nobody knows. It was many generations ago. He was a clever man, whoever he was, much more book learned than the people of his time. He found out something he should not have."

"What sort of thing? What did he find out?"

"We don't know. But it made him, the first in the family, terrified to be alone."

Impulsively I started to speak, then closed my mouth. I myself had just encountered that fear for the first time; I did not wish even to think of it.

"Has it ever occurred to you to wonder," said my grandfather, "what it would be like if you were alone in the world, in an empty room, in an empty house, in a deserted town; if you had reason to be certain that nowhere, not anywhere in the whole world, was there another living being?"

I had never thought of such a possibility. I did now, and shivered at the chill of it.

"There you are," said my grandfather, "waiting in the empty house, in the empty street, in the empty world. And yet, now, *something* comes and taps on the door."

I clutched his hand.

"How *can* it? What *is* that Something?"

"That Something," said my grandfather, "is what stands waiting, now, down in the deepest cellar of your mind."

I let out a sharp cry.

"No! It has no right! I won't have it! I can't bear it!"

"You have to bear it," said Grandfather. "There is no reason to suppose that you, out of the whole family, will be spared."

"Then I'll—I'll—I'll join the army. Like Father, like Peter."

But I knew I would not.

"No," he said. "You have to stay and work the smithy. With your mother's brothers."

"But what *is* the Something? Why is it so dreadful? Is it," I said hopefully, "is it just because we don't know what it is that it seems dreadful?"

"No," said Grandfather, quenching that hope. "It *is* dreadful. My dreams tell me that. It is dreadful, and it waits for all of us."

It has waited a long time for you, Grandfather, I thought. Ninety years.

And he spoke, echoing my thought.

"It has waited ninety years for me."

"But perhaps it won't ever get you, after all, Grandfather."

Flag whimpered dolefully at our feet, and Grandfather looked down and rubbed his ears.

"We must go home," he said. "It will be suppertime, and your mother will be wondering where you have got to."

"But what can I do about the—the thing, Grandfather? What can I do?"

"You can be brave," he said.

We walked back between the old houses with their gay flowers. Twilight was thickening in the air. My uncles had long done shoeing the cart horse, and the forge fire had been banked for the night; the tools were put away. I picked up my basket of dried, shriveled lily roots and trudged beside my grandfather in silence.

"Grandfather?" I said after a while.

"Well?"

"Why no imaginary friends?"

"Because," he said, "because, knowing your deep need, they could gain great power over you. And might in the end become the Terror themselves. You must learn to stand quite alone."

"I can't bear it," I said again, and he said again, "You have to bear it."

My grandfather died that night, quickly and quietly, in his sleep. Uncle Josef discovered him in the morning, cold and stiff already; lying straight in his bed for once, with his hands composedly crossed on his breast.

For three days I felt unbelievably wretched, as if my own two hands had been cut off at the wrist. Grandfather had told me so many things, had looked after me so long, had treated me more like a son than a grandson; how could I ever get along in life without him?

And then, too, there was the aching sense of guilt and worry; had I, with my questions and confessions, with my clamor and my need, somehow laid too heavy a load on him and so hastened his end?

But Father Tomas, the priest, told me that Grandfather was a man of sterling qualities, a brave, thoughtful, honest, generous man who died in the fullness of years; we should not grieve too much for him, but should be proud of his life and happy that he had gone to a better place.

This comforted me for a while.

We have this custom when somebody dies, that for

three days they lie in the church, on a stone bier, with the empty coffin waiting below. Then the priest blesses the coffin, and the burial takes place.

So it was with Grandfather. For three days he lay in the church. Every morning the people who had loved him came to cover his body with new flowers—asters and late roses and marigolds and trails of scarlet briony berries and bunches of golden cherry leaves. He looked like a warrior garlanded with wreaths of victory.

And during that time I thought, All is well with Grandfather.

But on the third night old Flag, who had lain for days like a stone dog, with his head on his paws, who would not eat or drink or let out any sound—on the third evening Flag began to howl. At the foot of the stairs he howled and howled, dementedly, until Uncle Josef said at last, "For God's sake, put the beast outside, this is not to be borne!"

So he was turned loose in the street and ran back and forth along the village all night, howling as if a pack of fiends were at his heels.

In the morning I found him crouched against the church door, shivering and whining. I tied him to a tree and raced to fetch Father Tomas, who unlocked the church door and went inside.

Waiting on the step, I heard him let out a great cry, and so I followed him into the church, my heart thudding.

There lay Grandfather on the stone floor, a whole man's length away from the bier. The dead flowers were scattered about him, some crushed beneath him.

He must have hurled himself off the stone table and clean over his coffin, which lay on the floor below.

He must have had another dream.

"But he was dead. He was *dead.* I should know, I have seen so many dead people. He has been dead for three days," Father Tomas kept repeating, and he crossed himself, over and over.

He sprinkled Grandfather's body with holy water, and the uncles came and helped him put it into the coffin. And nail down the lid.

The funeral was a hasty, furtive affair. Nobody looked at anybody else. Nobody spoke, apart from the usual prayers and psalms. And when it was over, the people dispersed to their own homes without the usual feast, without even loitering for conversation.

Back at home I huddled in a corner with my arms around old Flag and fed him bread dipped in honey and schnapps.

"What did he dream, old Flag? Do you know? Did he dream about Something?"

But old Flag only whined in reply.

I have a puppy now, one of his children's children, and he follows me wherever I go. And I am glad of his company, against the day, not too far now, I think, when it will be *my* turn to dream about Something.

Birthday Gifts

THE TWO SISTERS, Imelda and Catherine Dounraigh, had been, all their lives, in continual, if unavowed, competition. Ever since the early days, when their father, Professor Dounraigh, had addressed them impartially as Boots and Snooks and took no notice of either. The youngest son, Conor, was the only child in whom he showed the slightest interest; but unfortunately Conor, a brilliant boy, died untimely of Asian flu while in the senior class at Bramchester; his elder sisters, by now at Leeds and Durham universities respectively, were from then on completely ignored by their father, who withdrew, after that day, into a cloud of angry grief. Their mother's timid sympathy and partisanship had never been of the least importance to either of them; Mrs. Dounraigh, a gentle, unassuming person, had always been morally trampled underfoot by her husband, who, until the boy's death, had been a formidably successful mathematician. As a result of the tragedy, for which, in some obscure way he blamed her, she developed premature senility and had to be packed off into a home.

Imelda was of the opinion that her mother had done it on purpose.

"Mother was never anything but totally ineffectual," she used to say in her clipped, impatient way. "This is just her means of opting out."

From age five (when her brother was born) Imelda had regarded life as a kind of obstacle course in which it was incumbent on the entrants to vault higher, run faster, leap farther, than anybody else; if you did not do that, what was the point of it at all? She had taken an excellent degree in physics, switched over to biology, discovered an unknown genetic factor in weasels, and was now the acknowledged authority on a new and obscure form of computer virus.

She had always treated her sister, Catherine, with the same tolerant scorn accorded to her female parent. Father and Conor were the only ones who counted in the family. So it was a cause of genuine (if undisclosed) satisfaction that for some years Catherine's career seemed at a standstill; she appeared to be destined for the same kind of tame, domestic, undistinguished obscurity that had enmeshed their mother. After taking a moderate arts degree at Durham, she went on to a worthy but unremarkable art school, did nothing very notable there, and then retired to a cottage in East Anglia which had been bequeathed her by a sister of their mother's, and settled down to a life of what Imelda described as "the worst kind of boring, amateur rusticity. She makes *pots*, believe it or not, and *weaves*, and embroiders. It really is quite a waste. After all, when she was at school and university, she did have some kind of a *mind*."

Catherine's failure to marry had increased the gulf between the two sisters; Imelda, while still at university, had contracted an alliance with a brilliant chemist (who then went into politics by way of television) and proceeded to give birth to three highly intelligent children, who soon distinguished themselves at school and later in every possible way. The boys had medical careers, the girl took up dress design after gaining a first-class history degree.

When they were small, it had been convenient for their mother, during school vacations, to dispatch the children to their aunt Cathy in her rural retreat, where they could enjoy the advantages of riding and sea bathing, but after they were in their teens such contacts became a thing of the past; as ponies and windswept Suffolk beaches lost their appeal, visits to Aunt Cathy became condemned by Imelda's brood as boring. "Just an old cottage. Nothing to do in it." "What *does* she do with herself all day long?" her sister once asked with fascinated distaste. "*I* dunno. Reads, or embroiders in that studio of hers. We hardly see her."

It had never been inquired whether Catherine enjoyed the incursions of her niece and nephews; Imelda naturally assumed that the young people's visits would furnish an interesting and lively distraction to their aunt's quiet existence.

At last, intercourse between the sisters had been reduced to semiannual telephone conversations, during which Imelda, ringing up, would recount her family's latest triumphs in case Catherine had missed reading them in *The Times*: Graham's new job as Adviser to the Cabinet on the Distribution of Science Funds; her own honorary degrees from Adelaide, Tokyo, and Lausanne; Susannah's gold medal and commission to design clothes for small Royals; the boys' academic and professional successes.

Then, most unexpectedly, the balance tipped in the other direction: Catherine Dounraigh had spent, it seemed, the last ten years in researching, assembling, and processing the material for a monumental study of lethargy, which was published by Cambridge University Press and which received respectfully awestruck notices in the press. Not only was it acclaimed by scholars but the actual text was so witty, stylishly written, and absorbing that the book became, incredibly, a national best-seller, topped publishers' lists for weeks and months, was translated into Spanish, German, and Chinese, and made for its writer a substantial fortune, besides catapulting her into the public eye as an English picturesque country eccentric in the finest tradition. Catherine Dounraigh's Victorian cotton country dresses, rescued from East Anglian attics; her herb garden; her vegetarian cookery; the fact that her aunt, previous owner of the cottage, was reputed to have been a witch; her expertise on that obscure instrument, the baryton; her intelligent views on autism, hyperactivity, and other related topics, but, above all, her truly remarkable tapestries, a combination of paint, collage, and embroidery, were endlessly described, discussed, and portrayed in color supplements, TV programs, and journals of every caliber from *Private Eye* to *Goody Gumboots' Gossip Weekly.*

The tapestries were to be seen on view at Versailles, where they attracted so much acclaim that the Prado, the Cloisters, the Cluny, and several other museums were soon hotly engaged in outbidding one another (the Prado finally acquired them in the teeth of an anonymous Japanese bidder).

Imelda was at first, not unnaturally, somewhat stunned by all this celebrity and limelight focused so unexpectedly on her humdrum sister; but she appeared to take it graciously enough: "In our family we are all achievers, of course; except for poor mother; so it isn't at all surprising, really, that Catherine should produce something at last," she explained to various of her acquaintances who had expressed some surprise, remembering her frequent previous strictures and slighting references to "poor Cathy, Father used to say she was practically retarded, IQ barely normal." Whereas nowadays, recalling her father, Imelda tended to say, "He talked a great deal to me, latterly; I was the only one he *could* talk to, he used to say. Conor was bright, of course, but shallow; probably had one of those flash-in-the-pan brains that often fizzle out later. It may have been a mercy that he died when he did. Father would have been so disappointed if he hadn't fulfilled his early promise. Father always thought that Catherine might be a late starter. . . ."

Professor Dounraigh had died at the time of Imelda's marriage, so there was nobody to contradict these reminiscences.

Fortunately for Imelda, the balance was to some extent righted at this juncture by the publication of a book on Freud's obsession with maps, by Jonas, the elder of her two sons, both of whom had gone into popular psychiatry; while the daughter, Susannah, announced her engagement to the youngest son of a duke; so honors might have been considered even, except that the book on Freud was somewhat dismissively reviewed by several experts. "Shallow," "frothy," "lacking in depth" were comments calculated to give the mother of the writer no particular pleasure.

The sisters' birthdays, both in June, were only a week apart, and, when they were small, these anniversaries had, much to their annoyance, been, as a matter of convenience, celebrated together on a day midway between the two dates—as if they were not of sufficient importance to be considered worth taking separately. While Conor, whose birthday fell in October, had a festival all of his own.

It had been the sisters' habit, since they were grown, and possibly even before that, to give each other birthday presents that were ingeniously calculated to annoy. Clothes that were expensive, fitted well, but were unbecoming; records of composers known to be disliked; objets d'art so inappropriate as obviously to have been chosen out of malice or bought at charity sales; hideous foreign peasant artifacts; unreadable books. Once, three years in succession, Imelda had given her sister sets of lace-edged table doilies. "I don't use doilies, you know," Catherine had been driven to say on the third occasion. "Oh—don't you?" Imelda had answered vaguely. "I thought, somehow, that you did. . . ."

It was felt, tacitly, that she had scored a point on that anniversary in the unacknowledged duel that was forever being waged between them.

This summer Imelda's husband, Graham Klopstock (now Sir Graham), had suffered a mild lung infection and was ordered to take a rest in bracing sea air. His wife therefore proposed that the couple should come down to Suffolk for a week and the two sisters celebrate their birthdays together, a thing they had not done since their teens.

The plan may have had a certain basis in Imelda's wish to demonstrate to her acquaintances that she and her sister were on the most cordial of terms after the latter's unexpected fame, that envy or jealousy played no part in their relationship.

"Do you mean actually *stay* with your sister?" Sir Graham had demanded, in alarm. "No, no, *no*, we'll stay at the Walberswick Arms, of course, I don't know if Catherine even has a spare room anymore, the whole cottage is probably elbow-deep in art supplies and embroidery things. Characteristic of Catherine that if she had to take to an art form, it should be such a typically feminine one," remarked Imelda who, like her father before her, had a somewhat pejorative and puritanical attitude toward the arts.

So long as he was assured of residence at a comfortable hotel, Graham did not make any objections; his apprehensions had been raised by memories of his children's reports on Aunt Cathy's cottage "full of tables covered with typed pages and unfolded ironing boards with bits of material trailing everywhere." He had never been invited to the place himself, had indeed met his sister-in-law on only two other occasions: at his own wedding and at his father-in-law's funeral. (His mother-in-law, in her home, was still alive, but people tended to forget her existence for years together. A trust took care of her expenses.)

Surprised at the suggestion, but graciously assenting, Catherine booked a suite for the Klopstocks at the hotel and made arrangements to take them out to dinner on Imelda's birthday (which came first) at a local vegetarian restaurant of good repute. Neither of the visitors was a vegetarian. "But," as Catherine observed, "since I will have to come off my vegan diet for the meal, we are all making some concessions." "Of course," kindly assented Imelda, while Graham, looking depressed, said nothing.

"It really is a very lucky thing," added Catherine, "that you came down here for your birthday, since the present I found for you is so valuable that I should have hesitated to entrust it to the mail."

This gift turned out to be, when duly presented on the day, a Victorian nightdress of such amplitude, so tucked, rucked, frilled, ruched, adorned with *broderie anglaise* and insertions of narrow ribbon; so flounced, pounced, fringed, and trimmed; that it seemed made rather for some gigantic creation of antiquity, such as the Sphinx, than for human form.

"Thank you, my dear," faintly declared Imelda, whose taste for stark simplicity, based on the elegant fashions of her daughter, were, she fancied, well understood in the family.

"Knowing your fondness for lace-edged doilies, I knew it couldn't fail to please," Catherine blandly told her. "Besides, it has a most unusual and distinctive history. It belonged, believe it or not, to Florence Nightingale. The pedigree is absolutely authenticated. Nightingale gave it to an old and much-loved nurse, who retired here to Suffolk and never wore it but kept it as a family treasure. I thought, since you are such an advocate of women's advancement, that you would be specially interested in wearing a garment that had belonged to so notable a pioneer."

"I appreciate the thought very much."

"Mind you do wear it, now! You'll see that she does, won't you, Graham? This very night!"

"Certainly I will. Though," Imelda's husband added, bursting into laughter, "she will look just like a pregnant bracket fungus in it, won't you, darling?"

Imelda, tending to bony gauntness when young, had become, in middle age, almost square in shape; "having," as she impatiently said, "no time to indulge in all those self-preservative exercises with which some women seem to take up all their days."

She now studied the Victorian nightdress with silent dislike, wondering how soon it would be safe to give it either to her daughter, Susannah (though Susannah did not share the current trendy passion for such articles) or, preferably, to some folk museum. But would Catherine be likely to inquire after it? No use saying it had worn out. Its construction seemed guaranteed to defy time; it looked built to last forever.

Graham was vaguely wondering what kind of a garment his sister-in-law wore in bed. She was a strange-looking, eldritch little creature, with pointed features, wispy gray hair, and burning gray eyes; her clothes were amazingly nondescript but contrived to hang around her in picturesque folds, a feature that had been turned to full advantage by the Sunday color supplements. They looked as if they had been bought at rummage sales and doubtless had been; Graham decided that Catherine probably retired to bed in a man's flannel nightshirt.

Arrangements for her birthday were now under discussion. "The boys are bringing down your present," said Imelda. "It is to be a surprise. Con and Jonas have arranged it between them."

The boys, now two handsome successful young doctors in their early thirties, duly arrived on Catherine's birthday. (Susannah was unable to appear, being about to give birth to a ducal grandchild.) The whole party dined at the Walberswick Arms, Catherine eating nothing but grapefruit, undressed salad, and some of her own goat cheese which she had brought with her. She did, however, drink a little champagne.

Imelda was in a rather strange state; had been, indeed, for the last three days.

"For Christ's sake, Ma, what *is* it?" demanded Jonas as soon as he first laid eyes on her. "You look as if you've had a breakdown."

"I'm glad *someone* takes it seriously. Your father just thought it a load of nonsense. All *he* said was for heaven's sake don't talk about it to the P.M."

The P.M. was a great friend of Sir Graham and Lady Klopstock.

"He would," said Con. "But what *happened* to you?"

"It was that nightdress your aunt Cathy gave me for my birthday. I wore it that night. One night! If I'd slept in it again, I think I'd have died."

"For crying out loud! What did it do, give you dreams?"

"No, not dreams. Just moods, impressions. Utter, *utter* despair. Giving up. I could perfectly understand why Florence Nightingale retired to her bed and never got out of it again."

"She did quite a lot while she was *in* bed, mind," pointed out Jonas. "But still, I suppose in a way she did give up. Who else had the nightdress after her?"

"I don't know. But I'm sure whoever did just pined away and died of hopelessness."

"*Accidie*," said Con cheerfully. "One of the Seven Deadly Sins. What Aunt Cathy's an expert on. I must say, it was rather naughty of her to give it to you."

"Oh," said Imelda vaguely—she felt better now that she had been able to talk about her experience and have it discussed instead of laughed at—"very likely

Cathy didn't know about its effect. How should she? I don't suppose she wore it."

"I wonder," said Jonas, inspecting the garment. "Well, maybe we can try it on some of our patients. Be an interesting experiment."

He and his brother were now jointly running a clinic near Bury St. Edmunds for artistically creative psychotics—a picturesque venture that attracted a lot of publicity and funding.

"In the meantime you go and pick up Aunt Cathy for dinner, and Con and I will drop the present at her cottage after you've gone, so as to give her a surprise when she gets home. Then we'll follow you to the Arms for dinner."

This plan was duly carried out. The dinner was adequately festive, thanks to the high spirits of Jonas and Con, who teased their aunt in a fairly friendly way about her recent intellectual success.

"Number one on the best-seller list four months running! Put Ma's nose right out of joint. Hasn't it, Ma?"

Since Imelda's only published works were learned monographs on weasel genetics and computer viruses, this was regarded as a pleasantry and received with gracious humor.

After dinner they all adjourned to Catherine's cottage for coffee and liqueurs.

A wet June evening had succeeded a cold June day, and uneven shapes of misty rain wavered uneasily among the lilac, syringa bushes, and apple trees that screened Catherine's unassuming, grassy garden plot from the flat East Anglian landscape that lay beyond. It could not, as Jonas assured his brother in an undertone and with a nudge, have been better conditions for their surprise. Dark had not yet fallen—would not for another hour—but nobody could have said that the visibility was one hundred percent.

"Is that somebody upstairs?" said Imelda.

"Probably one of my cats," said Catherine.

"Here you are, Aunt Catherine," said Jonas, "a drop of Benedictine, just right for your vegan diet. Remember how you used to take us out gathering mussels when we were young and not health-conscious? My goodness me, Auntie, you certainly have some hardy and weatherproof friends! Who's *that*, out there in your garden?"

Catherine looked where he pointed and dropped her glass, which smashed on the flag stones.

The illusion was complete. It was only a dummy figure, cast in concrete, disposed on a metal office chair; but at a distance, through the wavering skeins of moist drizzle, against the mass of lilac bushes, it had exactly the appearance of a dead person. Or some aged, incapacitated figure, unable to get up and move. . . .

"It looks like *Conor*!" said Catherine, white to the lips. "How did—"

"No, it ain't, Aunt Cath! It's a model of Jonas there. Isn't it lifelike, though? Won't it make a conversation piece in your boring little garden? Just you wait, Auntie, till the color supplements see *him*!"

Young Con had fetched a dustpan and swept up the shards of glass. Catherine, with her color slowly coming back, was able to sip another drink and congratulate her relatives on a most original present.

"He weighs about a ton," said Con. "Don't try moving him yourself, Aunt Cath, or you'll slip a disk for sure. He'll be company for you out there! Just as good as a husband."

They all laughed.

"Even better," said Catherine, whose lips were still pale. "For I can always draw the curtains."

"He was made by one of our patients—a dear, sweet, creative fellow—only he *can* be rather naughty when the mood is on him. But he has a real gift for sculpture at other times. It's a great likeness of Jonas, isn't it?"

"I never noticed before," said Catherine, giving her nephew a slow scan, "how like your uncle Conor you are."

"Catherine must have detested her brother," said Sir Graham later, at the Walberswick Arms.

"Oh, no—I don't think so," answered his wife vaguely, taking off her glasses. "It's just that he was the only one to whom Father ever spoke."

After the Klopstock family had returned to town, Catherine Dounraigh made a strong and determined effort, which was on the whole successful, to ignore the piece of sculpture that occupied her garden.

The task was not easy. For the piece was quite large—slightly above life-size—and was so uncomfortably realistic. Rain or shine, there it sat, gray and patient in its metal chair, waiting. But for what? She might draw the curtains, but then it was still there, outside, waiting, whatever the weather. Lying in bed, she thought of it every night, sitting out there in the wet. She could have called in a neighboring farmer to remove it, with tractor and winch, drop it into one of the deep ponds for which Suffolk is well known—but that would be an admission of defeat.

Imelda had won another point, Catherine was obliged to acknowledge.

Moreover, as the months passed, Catherine observed something else, for which she could hardly give Imelda the credit.

Slowly, month by month, the concrete image was drawing closer to the house. For several weeks it would remain in the same spot—becalmed—and then one day she would discover that it had shifted, was a foot farther from the lilacs, a foot closer to the lily bed.

Autumn drew in, the dark fell earlier.

Catherine, who fortunately had learned method during her researches into the history of lassitude, now observed that the statue always seemed to make its move on the same night—a Sunday night before the first Monday in the month.

Armed with this useful and reassuring piece of solid fact, she kept impassive watch, concealed in a thick and screening clump of Dutch firs. And presently she was rewarded by the sight of her two nephews, parking their estate car in the adjoining stubble field and coming through the hedge with a jack and a trolley, evidently to move the statue, with a great many smothered chuckles.

One must pay this tribute to the Dounraigh family, thought Catherine: Even their practical jokes are carried out with fanatical efficiency, if on a somewhat juvenile level.

But when they approached more closely to the figure on the chair, she heard one of them let out a smothered shriek; and then they were both running for dear life to the boundary hedge, whimpering and moaning with fright.

Catherine stepped out from cover and impaled them with the brilliant beam of her police flashlight, ordering them to stop.

"Or I'll shoot!" she called.

Shamefaced, the brothers slowed to a standstill. A strong whiff of alcohol floated from them.

"Oh—it's you, Aunt Cath," Con gulped, mortally embarrassed.

"Whom did you think it was?"

"I—we—*that*—"

"A fine pair you are. Two doctors!" She looked at them scornfully. "You look like two twelve-year-olds. How long do you think it took me to work out that you visit the clinic at Saxingby on the first Monday of every month? You ought to be ashamed of yourselves. How would you like this to get into the papers?"

"Aunt Cath—" Jonas glanced behind him. "Who the *hell* have you got sitting on that chair?"

Catherine glanced toward the chair. The figure on it—now voluminously robed in some kind of white enveloping garment—had risen cumbrously to its feet and taken one or two slow paces toward them. Jonas let out another little whine of terror—he was plainly the more inebriated of the two—bolted through the scanty hedge, and disappeared from view. A moment later they heard the sound of the motor starting.

"He's got no guts at all, has he?" said Catherine acidly. "At least you didn't run, Con. Don't you want to come and meet your grandmother?"

With his legs barely supporting him, Con lurched forward until he could get a focused view of the massive figure, wrapped in pale fur, with its blurred features and melancholy puzzled eyes.

"I've had her living with me for the past year and a half," said Catherine. "Take her arm, will you, Con; that's right. And she's a lot better now—aren't you,

Mother?—than she was at the start. Shall we go back to the house now, Mother?"

"Yes, dear; if you say so. . . ."

The body of Jonas, still in his car, was found at the bottom of one of the deep Suffolk ponds next day. Catherine felt badly about that. She had not anticipated such a drastic outcome. But, as he had been the one to plan the practical joke with the statue, she felt that the blame for his death must be at least partly his own.

The two sisters never communicated again. But Mrs. Dounraigh made a modest recovery under her daughter's patient care and is now able to read large type, embroider, and knit.

The Rose-Garden Dream

My brother Skid can do this queer thing.

Could do.

He only did it twice, that I know of; but twice is twice more than probably any other person in the whole world.

And I've dreamed of him doing it other times. And I think sometimes my dreams of him are true. Can't say for sure, as I haven't seen him since he left home. He don't write to me, and I don't write him, for I've no address to send to.

Skid can just *go*. . . .

Of course there has to be a mirror in the room or a bowl of water. Something that reflects.

The first time he done it, was when we were in grade school. We're twins, see, that's why we dream the same dreams. "What happened after we walked in the door?" Skid'd say, putting on his socks in the morning, and I'd say, "Don't you remember? We looked about and saw the wallpaper was all blue and white flowers," and he'd say, "Oh, yes, now I got it."

Of course our best dream, the one we had regular, it might be as often as twice a month, was the Garden of Roses dream. We never tired of that one. And Skid didn't need reminding about it; I reckon we both of us just about know it by heart.

It never changed, see.

Anyway, back to grade school. Herdman Road Infants, it was. I started there six weeks before Skid, 'cause he got asthma very bad and had to stay home. He was always getting asthma, and it used to rile Dad. He said Skid could easily snap out of it if he—— ——chose. Our elder brothers didn't get asthma, why should he? Dad used to get very mad and slap him about. Nothing to what he done later, though.

So, anyway, I'd got used to the school six weeks before Skid turned up, and that wasn't a bad thing; I knew, and I could tell him, which doors to go through, things like that, which of the big ones was horrible, which weren't so bad as they looked, and which teachers to keep clear of.

Bad luck for Skid, he got there three days before our birthday.

Girls didn't have it as bad on their birthdays. But with the boys, for some reason, Mr. Goadby (he was one to keep clear of), he used to make the birthday kid come out in front of his class and then, don't ask me why, he'd pull the kid's hair and ears, and thump him on the head with a Bible. Thumped really hard too. All meant in fun, he *said*, but lots of the boys hated it, some of them yelled.

And, when I told Skid what he had to expect, I could see he was dreading it. Really dreading it. He was little and skinny, covered in bruises anyway because of our dad having it in for him at home, and he was timid.

Things like that upset him more than they done other boys.

So, on our birthday, going to school, he was white as Wonder Bread already, and I could see the beads of sweat all over his spotty, scurfy little forehead.

"Does it happen right away?" he asked, licking his lips as if they were flaky dry.

"Can't tell," I says. "Sometimes first thing. Sometimes old Goader takes a fancy to do it at the end of the period. But don't you be scared, boy. Just stand there, don't show him you're bothered. 'Cause then he only goes on more. Remember, now!"

"Come out there, now, the birthday lad!" roars out Goadby, halfway through, and I was glad for Skid so he'd get it over with.

A couple of others pushed him out from the boys' side of the room, and he stood in front, flinching, sort of, and squinting sideways up at Goadby, who's tall and bony and redheaded.

"Ah, yes. Our dear little Skidmore Weatherby. A most distinguished patro-nymic," says Goadby, kind of smacking his lips and glowering at the same time. "Pity you don't *look* the part more, eh? Eh? *Stand up straight, boy!*" he suddenly barked, and made Skid start so much, he nearly fell over, and the current of air, when he jumped, must have affected a small round shaving mirror what was dangling on a string from the ceiling (for some project the bigger ones had been doing) and it turned slowly around, flashing as it caught a ray of the sun, then tipping lopsided so it happened to catch Skid's terrified eye as he gazed upward, waiting for the punishment to begin.

And—suddenly—he wasn't there.

Goadby had looked away for a second, when the

flash from the mirror caught *his* eye. And when he looked back, Skid was gone.

"Hey, *you*! Come back!" bawls Goadby. "I hadn't finished with you yet. Devil take it, where *is* the brat? Where's he hiding? Who's sheltering him? Come out from under that desk, I can see you!"

He prowled all over the classroom (it wasn't very big) while we all sat paralyzed. *Nobody* was going to say, "Skid took and vanished" because, for a start, we didn't believe it ourselves. Things like that just don't happen. And, secondly, if anyone was such a clunch as to say it, he'd have had Goadby down on him like the Last Trump.

So we sat mum and mute and squinted at each other out of the corners of our eyes. And presently, looking out the window, Goadby says, "Why, there *is* the little beggar, out there in the playground. That boy will grow into a cat burglar. How did he get out there? I never saw a getaway to beat it. Go out there and fetch him back, Blaydon."

But luckily at that moment the bell rang for end of period, and we all ran off, and even Goadby didn't try to take it any farther.

I said to Skid in the playground, "What *happened*?"

He was looking dazed. He said, "I dunno. I was lookin' in the glass—we was both lookin' in the glass, him an' me—an' I could see the playground in the glass as well, over his shoulder, like—an' then I was *there*. Out there. In the playground."

"You didn't go through the door?"

"Don't remember," he said, looking doubtful.

I could tell he didn't like being asked about it. We didn't say anything about it to Mam, and we *certainly* didn't tell our dad. And as no one at school believed what they'd seen, no one talked about it after that.

Skid never done well at school, and his asthma got worse. And he used to get terrible pains in the belly and couldn't eat. That made Dad really wild. "If you don't eat your dinner today," he used to tell Skid, "then you'll get it tomorrow. And so on till you do finish it." Breathing heavily down on the kid, smelling of beer. Sometimes the same plate of stew would come out, day after day, till it got to look really nasty, kind of wrinkled and buckled and grainy, as if at any moment the whole plateful might begin to heave about. It made you gulp just to see it. Mam wasn't much of a cook at best. And nobody's stew is up to much after four days.

So one afternoon Skid was stuck in the back kitchen with a plate of stuff like that. Mam couldn't stand it—our dad was just as hard on her as on the rest of us—and she'd gone down the yard with a basket of wash to hang up.

"Now: I'm going upstairs to get my Sunday belt," says Dad—his Sunday belt was the one he used to tan us with, 'cause it was thicker—"I'm going to get my Sunday belt and if that stew's not et up by the time I'm back, my boy, you're going to be sorry. Very sorry."

He walked up the stairs, slow and heavy. Skid gave a kind of panic-stricken stare around our back kitchen. Brick floor, table, chairs, sink. Our row of boots by the back door. Quick as a flash, Skid poured the plate of stew (it was quite runny) into his boots. He done it very neat, considering. There was just enough to fill both boots. They weren't very big. Then he's at the table again, sitting in front of the empty plate, when Dad comes back.

I was rinsing socks under the tap, sick with fright.

Dad looks at the plate and does a double take.

"You never et that in the time, boy, don't try to fool me," he says, and his eye roams slowly around the room, kettle on the stove, old Jip in his dog basket, clock on the mantel, calendar on the wall. Then it comes to the boots.

"Aha!" says Dad as if satisfied. "Thought you'd be one too many for me, did you, young man? Well—I'm about to show you that you are WRONG!"

He starts off slow and quiet, but ends on a shout, with his face dark red, and beery breath coming quick.

Skid sits at the table, petrified.

"Get out o' the way, you," Dad says, elbowing me away from the sink, and he fills the washing-up pan with water and sets it on the table. Then he picks up one of the boots full of cold stew.

"Now, my boy," he says, walking slow toward Skid, "you are going to swallow down this stew, if I have to tip it all down your skinny throat. Then you are going to swallow what's in the other boot. And then you are going to wash those boots—your good boots, what cost money—in that pan of water. And *then* you are going to get such a tanning—"

As he moved toward Skid, I saw my brother's eyes shoot wildly about the kitchen and come to rest on the pan of water. It reflected the sky, and the branches of the big old cherry tree in the yard.

Next moment Skid's gone. Like a pricked bubble.

There's Dad, standing by the table, with the boot full of stew in his hand, looking dumbstruck.

Next minute we hears a shriek, and something big and dark falls past the window. I hear Mam's voice outside in the yard calling, "Bert! Bert! Sal! Come quick! Skid's fallen! He's hurted himself! *Quick!*"

"What the—— —— ——!" says Dad; and, after a moment or two, staring about him as if he's just come out from under gas, he stumbles out the back door.

I take the chance, while there's no one about, to tip the stew from both boots into Jip's tin dinner pan. Jip gives me a grateful look and starts in eating it in big gulps. (Jip's always raving hungry and not particular.) I rinse Skid's boots in the pan of water and run out after Dad.

He and Mam are having a big stand-up argument.

"I saw him fall, I tell you!" she yells at him. "Out of the cherry tree! Go and fetch the doctor. Hurry! He may have busted something. I'm not shifting him till the doctor's seen him. Very like he's got concussion. Look at the way he lies!"

Then I saw Skid, flat out in the grubby flower bed full of snail shells outside the kitchen window where Mam tries to grow mint and parsley. Skid didn't move at all. And one of his arms was doubled back in a queer way.

"What *I* want to know is," said Dad, "how the—— blazes did he get there when he was indoors just now?"

"How should *I* know?" says Mam, short and wild. "Maybe you throwed him there." And, under her breath, I hear her mutter, "One o' these days you'll go too far—"

Dad, looking angry and 'mazed, goes for the doc. Who says that Skid's got concussion and a busted arm. So he's in bed for a bit; and the boots and the stew's not spoken of, though we all know Dad'll have it in for Skid even worse when he does get up.

* * *

"What happened *that* time?" I ask Skid a couple of days later, one evening when we're alone in the bedroom, Mam and Dad down the pub.

"I saw the tree's branches . . . in the water . . . and next minute I was *in* them. That's all. I don't want to talk about it," says Skid. "Let's talk about our garden."

So we talked about that instead.

It's always the same, our dream. First, walking up the path to this mountain. Steep path, rocky, spiky mountain. Blue and bony against the pale sky. Then we get to the gates. There's four of 'em, all gold, solid gold. Big and splendid, flashing. Like the gates to a palace. Higher than your head. Funny thing, there's no fence. Just a silk thread, running from one pair of gates to the next. You'd think *anybody* could get in. But they can't, only us. There's something queer about that thread. Maybe it's electrified. No one can get past it. You touch it, your hand comes off. Or whatever you touched it with. "I wish Dad would touch it," Skid said once, kind of dreamy.

But, mostly, when we are there, we don't think about anything at home.

We go through one of the gates, it don't matter which, they open for us as we come to them, like the doors of the Welcome Supermarket. And then we're inside. First thing you notice is the scent of the roses. They're everywhere, huge, tall rose trees, higher than houses, all covered with big, open roses, wide open and sweet smelling. Not the kind you see at Green Alley Florist's, tight and narrow and wrapped up with no scent to 'em; these ones have a big, open patch of gold in the middle, round as an eye, and the scent's enough to turn you giddy.

There's narrow paths winding everywhere among the big old rose trees, and birds singing. Not birds we know, foreign ones, and you can't see 'em, but their voices are loud and sweet; they're all singing their hearts out.

Skid and I wander about in there—sometimes it seems like hours, sometimes only five or ten minutes. Then, slowly, a cold mist comes along the paths, and the bushes begin to dim away into it, and the birds' voices aren't so loud, and then—all of a sudden—it's gone, and we're outside in the cold. And I can't find words to tell *how* cold and sad that is. For each time we're there, we believe that *this* time we'll be able to stay and not ever, ever go back.

But of course we never can.

"Someday I will, though," says Skid. "Someday I'm going to pick one of the roses. If we could only do that, I reckon we could get to stay."

"Roses are hard to pick. You need scissors or clippers. Or a knife."

"Well, I'll take one." And for a while Skid took to hiding a little penknife under his pillow, one our brother, Bob, gave him for Christmas. But it never works. When we have our rose-garden dream, the knife stays behind, at home, under the pillow.

And maybe, I think, that's just as well. For if Skid managed to pick one of the roses, it might work the other way. It might break the spell. He might never get back to the garden again.

Our garden never changed. But we changed. We got bigger, and Dad got angrier. Time we got to fifteen, Dad was laying into Skid just about every time they was together. Hurt him real bad sometimes.

So in the end Skid run off.

What else could he do?

There's no jobs around where we live, so he couldn't have got one anyway. It's a case of signing on and lining up. That's all they ever do. Skid couldn't stand for that, not and then come home to be knocked about by our dad. So he run off, up to the big city.

I reckon so, at least. That's what he said he'd do. And I often dream about him. I can see him trudging about the streets; he looks thin and pale, with his fair hair getting longer and greasier. Mostly he's hungry, got nothing to eat. Skid wouldn't mind that part of it too much, for he never did eat a lot. But I worry, 'cause he's getting *ever* so thin.

And at night I see him and all the other kids— sometimes there's scores of 'em—lying under these arches, if it's wet weather, or along by the river, under a bridge. Some of 'em has newspapers wrapped around, some has sleeping bags; more has nothing at all.

Night after night I get this dream of Skid and all the others, most of them as young as him, lying there side by side, like sardines, under the greeny, greasy light of the streetlamp.

Sometimes Skid is dreaming our dream. And sometimes I dream it too; but not so often now. More often, now, I'm dreaming about *him*.

So, one night, along the street comes this old guy. He's blind, you can tell, for he has a white stick, ivory, with a silver handle, and he goes tap, tap. But he's well dressed, quite grand, in a coat with a fur collar, and a hat, and has another big feller with him, who seems like a servant. You can tell. They go along, slow, looking down at all the sleepers lined up along the pavement.

Every now and then the one with the stick stops and gives a poke to one o' the sleepers, and says to him, "Quick: tell us what you are dreaming about!"

And, mostly, the sleeping guy will wriggle and curse and mumble some rubbish, or just growl, "Go to hell! Leave me be!" and then the two wakeful ones will go on their way.

But every now and then one of the sleepers will say something that makes the big feller snap on a tape recorder he carries on a strap around his neck. And then they listen real careful.

And so they come along, and they get to Skid.

Skid is sleeping very peaceful and, right away, I know he's dreaming the rose-garden dream. I can tell it by the happy look on his face and the way he lies, his hands relaxed, breathing so quietly. And when the guy touches him with his stick and says, "Quick! Tell me what you are dreaming!" Skid rolls onto his back and begins to talk, in a clear voice and very fast, on and on, as if he's one of those radio announcers giving the forecast. But what he says is just gibberish, not even English, but a kind of nonsense language: "Abana teapotty throumi tirpan weeho," or something just as crazy as that. Whatever it is, the big guy snaps on his tape recorder and catches it all. And the blind guy seems to get very excited, and by and by wakes Skid by giving him a sharp poke with the ivory cane.

"Hey! Don't *do* that!" yells Skid, looking up, confused and blinking, at the two above him. "Why the plague did you have to wake me? Who are you? I wasn't doing anything wrong."

"No, no, of course not," says the blind guy. He

speaks very posh and calm, like a TV news commentator. "And we don't mean you any harm."

"Well, then, leave me alone!"

Skid is sore, because of being woke from his dream. I can see that.

"I'd like you to come to my studio," says the blind guy. "It's just along here. We'll give you a bit of supper. And there's money in it for you. Come along with us, now."

They've got a car, a big old Rolls, and somehow they manage to coax Skid into it. Next thing I see them bring him into this big room, with a huge, high ceiling, and window looking out over the river. "This used to be what's-his-name's studio," says the blind guy. Some name like Rosy. Didn't mean nothing to me, nor to Skid, who was looking sort of scared and panicky.

"What d'you *want* with me?" he keeps saying. "Leave me alone!"

"No harm, I promise. I'm doing research," says the blind guy, soothing as the doctor when he's going to stick a big, dirty needle in your backside. And, in fact, when they give Skid a sandwich and a glass of Coke, I see the big bloke slip a shot of something into the Coke, out of a little bottle. And very soon Skid starts to fall asleep, lying back on a kind of sofa they call a shay zlong. Up on the wall at the end of the room is a huge old silvery mirror that shows the river outside, and tugboats and police launches going past.

You can feel it's very late, after midnight.

"Just lie back now, comfortable," says the blind guy, and, for the third time, he says "We don't mean you any harm."

"What *do* you want, then?" mumbles Skid, and the guy says, "I collect dreams, that's all."

"Well, you're not going to collect mine!" shrieks Skid, suddenly wide awake and panicking. "My dream's all I ever had, and *you're not getting it off me!"* —and suddenly he's gone, clean out of the room, and the two guys looking at each other, utterly scared and shook and puzzled, like Dad or Mr. Goadby back in Herdman Road Infants. There's nothing between them but the empty leather sofa.

So what I see next is people on the riverbank, pulling something ashore. There's cops, and torches, and the splash of water and thump of oars against concrete piling.

And there's Skid, laid out on the bank, white and wet and silent in the blue light of the police lamp. Dead as a mackerel on a fishmonger's slab.

And in his clenched fingers is a big pink open rose.

All this is only my dream! All this is only my dream!

Watkyn,
Comma

When Miss Harriet Sibley, not in her first youth, received an unexpected legacy from a great-uncle she had never met, there was not a single moment's hesitation in her mind. I shall give up my job at the bank, she thought and live by making cakes.

Miss Sibley had never baked a cake in her life, nor was she even a great cake eater; once in a while, perhaps, she might nibble a thin slice of Madeira, or a plain rice bun; but rice buns were becoming exceedingly hard to find.

All the more reason why I should start up a little baking business, thought Miss Sibley triumphantly. I need not have a shop. I can do it from home. Word about good cakes very soon gets passed around.

And she began hunting for suitable premises.

Due to soaring house prices, she encountered considerable difficulty in finding anything that lay within her means. For months every Saturday and Sunday was passed in the search. From cottages she turned to warehouses, from warehouses to barns. Even a ruined barn, these days, fetched hundreds of thousands.

But at last she came across exactly what she wanted, and the price, amazingly, was not unreasonable. Miss Sibley did not waste any time investigating possible disagreeable reasons for this; if there are drawbacks, I will deal with them as they come up, she decided, in her usual swift and forthright way, and she made an offer for the ruins of Hasworth Mill. Her offer was instantly accepted, and she engaged a firm of local builders to render the ruins habitable.

The building stood on a small island, with the river Neap on one side, describing a semicircle, and the mill-race on the other, spanned by a three-arched bridge.

What better place to bake cakes than a mill? thought Miss Sibley.

When she inquired why the place had remained uninhabited for so long, she received a variety of answers. The mill itself had ceased to grind corn after the closure of Hasworth Station and its branch railway line, which had made the transport of corn and flour so much more costly. Then there had been legal disputes between the heirs of the last owner. One had been in Canada, one in Australia; the affair had dragged on for years. Meanwhile the damp rotted the woodwork as the mill stood empty. Purchasers don't like damp, Miss Sibley was told. But damp is, after all, to be expected if you live on an island, she replied sensibly. Then there were the trees, very large: a huge cedar, twice the height of the mill, guarded the approach bridge; some willows grew on the island; a row of Lombardy poplars screened the meadow beyond. Trees make a place dark; some people dislike it.

Miss Sibley had lived all her life on a brick street;

to her the prospect of owning twelve Lombardy poplars, five willows, and a giant cedar was intoxicating.

The word *haunted* never passed anyone's lips.

The island itself was small; not much bigger than a tennis court. During the years that the mill had stood empty, brambles had proliferated and the place was a wilderness; Miss Sibley looked forward to turning it into a garden by and by. Meanwhile the builders used it as a dumping place for their loads of bricks and stacks of new timber. The brambles were cut and trampled down, and some of them dug up as new drains had to be laid and damp-proof foundations inserted; in the process of this digging a male skeleton was unearthed.

It had been buried with care, and quite deep, handsomely coffined and wrapped in some half-rotted piece of brocade material, which Dr. Adams, the coroner, who was also a keen local historian, inspected carefully and pronounced to be the remains of an altar cloth or consecrated banner.

"In fact, my dear Miss Sibley, the body is probably that of a Catholic priest who died here while on an undercover mission during Queen Elizabeth's reign and was secretly buried. The age of the remains make that the most likely hypothesis."

"But why should he be buried on my island?" crossly demanded Miss Sibley.

"Why, Jeffrey Howard, the miller at that period, had been suspected of being an undeclared papist. This seems to confirm it. Perhaps he was giving hospitality to one of the traveling priests who rode about in disguise, saying a secret Mass here and there. I suppose there was some fatality. That would account—" began Dr. Adams, and stopped short.

"So what happens now?" inquired Miss Sibley, not noticing this.

"Oh, we'll have him reburied properly in the graveyard, poor fellow," said Dr. Adams cheerfully. "The vicar won't mind a bit. He'll enjoy an excuse for some research into the background of it all."

Once the coffin and its melancholy contents had been removed, Miss Sibley put the matter out of her mind. She was much too busy, buying curtain material and discussing fitments with the builders to trouble her head about old unhappy far-off things. Her new kitchen was taking shape, a fine, spacious room with a view through dangling willow fronds over the white, frothy, and turbulent millpond. The sun blazed through the wide new south window, her large modern oven would soon keep the kitchen warm and airy.

Miss Sibley had a deep trunk full of cake recipes which, all her life, she had been cutting out of newspapers. She could hardly wait to get started. Waffles, Aberdeen butteries, orange and walnut cake, tipsy cake, scruggin cake, apricot-caramel cake, mocha layer cake, Tivoli cake, orange tea bread, date shorties, fat rascals, cut-and-come-again cake, honey and walnut scone ring, Lancashire wakes cakes, nut crescent, currant roll-ups, rum baba—these names sang themselves through her head like a glorious invocation.

Just wait till I can get the builders out of here, she thought. And shelves put up in the little room and my cookery books on them.

She had collected cookbooks with the enthusiasm of an autograph hunter. Not a recipe had yet been tried.

To encourage them, Miss Sibley pampered her builders in every way possible. She brewed them cups of tea five or six times daily, accompanied by store bought biscuits. She mailed letters, took messages, phoned their wives, and ran errands for them. But none of this disguised her extreme impatience to see them leave. As soon as it was at all possible, she planned to move from her rented room over the post office into the mill; meanwhile she visited the site daily and dug up brambles on the island. She was therefore on hand when Mr. Hoskins, the foreman, came to say, "Beg your pardon, mum, but we found something you should see."

"And what is that?" asked Miss Sibley. The seriousness of his tone made her heart tip over most anxiously. What could the wretches have found *now*? A plague pit? A cavern under the foundation, requiring ninety tons of concrete? Some terrible gaping crack that would entail construction of five expensive brick buttresses?

"It's a room," said Mr. Hoskins.

"A room? A *room*? Surely there are plenty of those?"

"One we didn't know of," replied Mr. Hoskins, who had lived in the village all his life. "Halfway up a wall. Come and see, mum."

Her curiosity kindled, Miss Sibley came and saw.

The room was approached by a paneled door, neatly concealed at one side over the mantel in a small upstairs bedroom. The panel door was operated by a hidden spring, which one of the workmen had accidentally released. Inside, a flight of narrow dark stairs led up to a small, low, irregularly shaped chamber with a sloped ceiling and several oak beams passing through the floor at odd angles. The place was not much larger than a coat closet and was dimly lit by a tiny window, made of thick greenish glass tiles, which also admitted a little fresh air.

"Why has nobody ever noticed the window?" demanded Miss Sibley.

" 'Tis hid by the ivy, you see, mum, and also 'tis tucked in under the overhang of the eaves, like, where you'd never notice it," Mr. Hoskins pointed out.

Later, going outside, Miss Sibley verified this, and the fact that a projecting lower gable concealed the window from anyone standing on the ground.

Disappointingly the room held no furniture.

"But we did find this," said Mr. Hoskins, and handed Miss Sibley a small grimed leather-bound book. " 'Twas tucked on the joist."

Opening the book, Miss Sibley found that the pages were handwritten. It seemed to be a diary.

"Thank you, Mr. Hoskins," she said.

"Would you want the room decorated, miss?"

"On the whole, no, thank you, Mr. Hoskins. I don't imagine I shall be using it a great deal. If you could just clear away the dust. . . ."

Miss Sibley's mind was already floating back to Sicilian chocolate cheesecake.

But she did take a cursory glance at the diary, which was written in a faded brown ink and a decidedly crabbed and difficult handwriting.

"I, Gabriel Jerome Campion, S.J., leave this journal as a memorial in case it should happen that I do not quit this place a living man. And I ask whomsoever shall find it to pray for the repose of my soul. . . ."

Well, of course I will do that for the poor man, thought Miss Sibley, and she methodically tied a knot in her handkerchief to remind herself.

I wonder if he was in here for very long, and what did happen to him?

"Thank you, Mr. Hoskins," she repeated absently, and withdrew down the narrow approach stair to the builders' stepladder, which stood below the panel opening.

"Would you wish me to put a different fastening on the door, mum?"

"Why, no, thank you, I think the existing one will do well enough."

"Or build a flight of steps so's to reach the door?"

"No," said Miss Sibley, "as you may recall, I plan to turn this little bedroom into my cookery library, so I shall want shelves built across those two facing walls for my cookbooks. And then, you see, I'll buy one of those little library stepladders, so if I ever should wish to enter the secret room (which is not very likely), I can use the stepladder. Thank you, Mr. Hoskins. Gracious me—it is teatime already; I'll just run and put on the kettle."

Dr. Adams and Mr. Wakehurst the vicar were greatly excited by the discovery of the diary, news of which reached them that evening by village grapevine; and the next day Mr. Wakehurst came around to ask if he might borrow the document?

"This, you know, clears up a four-hundred-year-old mystery," said he, happily. "There is a local legend about a black-coated stranger who was heard asking the way to Hasworth Mill and was then never seen again. But that was the winter of the great flood, when the Neap overran its banks and covered all the land as far as the foot of Tripp Hill (where the deserted station now stands). Various people from the village were drowned in the floods, including Howard the miller. It was supposed that the stranger must have been drowned, too, and his body washed downstream to Shoreby. Now we can guess that he had been billeted in the secret room by Howard, who no doubt proposed to see him off the premises when the coast was clear; but because of his death in the flood he never did return. So the poor priest probably starved to death. Howard's son, a sailor who returned from the sea to claim his inheritance, no doubt found and secretly interred the body. Poor fellow, what a miserable, lonely end."

"Oh, he wasn't lonely," said Miss Sibley. "Somebody called Mr. Watkyn kept him company. He wrote, several times, in his diary, 'I don't know how I should have managed to remain tranquil and composed without the company of my dear and charming Watkyn.'"

"Indeed?" exclaimed the vicar, with the liveliest curiosity. "Now I *do* wonder who Watkyn can have been?"

"Another priest, I daresay," remarked Miss Sibley without a great deal of interest, and she handed Mr. Wakehurst the fragile and grimy little volume. "Please do keep it, Vicar, it is of no great interest to me."

"May I really? I shall write a paper on it for the Wessex Archaeological Society," cried the vicar joyfully, and hastened away with his treasure before she could change her mind.

At the door he turned, remembering his manners, to ask, "When do you plan to move in, Miss Sibley?"

"Why, tonight," said she. "There are still quite a few things to be done, but the kitchen stove works now, and the hot water is on, and one of the bedrooms is finished, so there is no reason why I can't sleep here.

That way I shall be even more on the spot if there are any problems—not that I anticipate any."

Mr. Wakehurst's face wore a slightly doubtful, frowning look as he crossed the three-arched bridge and looked down at the careering millrace and swirling millpond. But what, after all, are ghosts? he thought. Some people never see them at all. And, as the century nears its end, they seem to be losing their power. And Miss Sibley is such a sensible, practical person, it would be a most unpardonable piece of folly to confuse her mind with ideas about things that may never happen.

Poor Father Gabriel! As good a man as ever stepped, I daresay, even if he did hold erroneous, wrongheaded religious opinions. In any case, we are all so much more ecumenical and broad-minded now.

I do wonder who Watkyn can have been? And why no other body was found? Dear me, how very, very interested Adams will be in this discovery.

Besides, nobody has actually *seen* anything in the mill. Or not that I have been told of. It is only some exaggerated stories about what people felt, or fancied they felt, or heard, or fancied they heard.

He hurried on, under a threatening and plum-colored sky, absorbed by the diary, which he read as he walked.

"Conducted a long dialogue on transubstantiation with Watkyn, which served to distract me from the pangs of hunger. His is a surpassingly sympathetic and comprehending nature. And his expression is so captivatingly cordial! If he chose, I know that he would confide in me all his innermost thoughts."

Can Watkyn have been a mute? wondered Mr. Wakehurst. Or a foreigner, speaking no English?

"I have confessed to Watkyn not only my major transgressions but the most minor peccadilloes, the kind of small sins that, in the presence of a confessor, one is often almost ashamed to mention. Watkyn, now, knows more of my faults than any other living being. He does not behave any less kindly. And I feel a wondrous easement of soul. Sick, enfeebled, confused as I begin to grow, I do not at all fear to meet my Maker. And it is all thanks to my good Watkyn. If only I could bestow a like grace on him!"

"Another discussion with W. on the subject of miracles," recorded Father Gabriel a day later, in a hand that was perceptibly weaker.

Now, what in the world can have become of Watkyn? wondered the vicar.

"Talked to W. on the subject of Redemption . . ." The text trailed away.

Miss Sibley celebrated her first night of residence in Hasworth Mill by making a Swiss roll. Not surprisingly it was a total disaster. What she had thought to be one of the most simple, basic, and boring of cakes is, on the contrary, the most tricky and delicate, on no account to be attempted by a beginner. The flour must be of a special kind, the eggs carefully chosen, the oven well trained, familiar to the cook, and under perfect control. Not one of these factors obtained at the mill. It was the first time Miss Sibley had used her new oven, which was not yet correctly adjusted; the flour was damp and in any case not a good brand. The eggs were a mixed lot. The cake turned out sodden, leathery, and had to be scraped from the bottom of the pan, like badly laid cement. Not surprisingly, after eating a mouthful or two, Miss Sibley went to bed very quenched and dejected and then found it almost impossible to fall asleep in her bare and paint-scented bedroom.

A gusty and fidgety wind had blown up. As Miss Sibley sat after supper in her warm kitchen, she could see, through the great pane of clear glass, long, dangling fronds of the willows in wild and eldritch motion, blown and wrung and swung like witches' locks. And after she retired to bed, her high window, facing out over the water-meadow, showed the row of Lombardy poplars like a maniac keep-fit class, violently bowing and bending their slender shafts in each and every direction.

Miss Sibley could not hear the wind, for, to anybody inside the mill house, the roar of water drowned out any external sound. But as the gale increased, she *could* hear that, somewhere within the house a door had begun to bang; and after ten minutes or so of increasing irritation she left her bed to find the source of the annoyance and put a stop to it.

The offending door proved to be the one opening into her little library room.

Queer, thought Miss Sibley; the window in here is shut; why should there be a draft? Why should the door bang?

And then she noticed the high black square in the wall, the cavity where the panel door stood open. That's very peculiar, she reflected. I'm sure Mr. Hoskins had left it closed when the men went off work, and *I* certainly haven't opened it, so how in the world could it have come open all by itself? But perhaps this wild and drafty wind somehow undid the catch. At any rate I may as well close it up again; it is letting a nasty lot of cold air into the upper story.

Since the panel door and its catch were too high for

her to reach, she pushed a table, which she proposed to use as a writing desk, across the small room, perched a chair on the table, and then climbed up onto the chair.

She was in the act of closing the door when she thought she heard, from inside the little upper room, a faint and piteous moan. She paused, listened harder, but there was no repetition of the sound.

I was mistaken, decided Miss Sibley. She closed the panel, climbed down from the table, and was about to return to bed, when, from inside the panel, came three, loud, measured knocks.

Bang. Bang. Bang.

Then a moment's silence. Then the three knocks again.

Bang. Bang. Bang.

Can that be the wind? Miss Sibley wondered and, after a moment's hesitation and just a little nervous this time, she climbed up onto the table once more, reopened the door, and peered inside. There was nothing to be seen.

But again, after the door was shut, before she had left the room, she heard the three knocks: Bang. Bang. Bang.

"This is perfectly ridiculous," said Miss Sibley angrily. "However, I certainly can't lie all night listening to those thumps, so I suppose I shall have to investigate further. But I'm not going dressed like this."

Accordingly she returned to her bedroom, pulled on a pair of trousers and thick cardigan, and equipped herself with a powerful flashlight, which she had bought in case of any trouble with the newly installed electrical system. Once again she climbed onto the table, and this time scrambled right up into the panel entrance.

No sooner was she well inside the entrance than the door swung violently closed behind her and latched itself. She heard the spring click into place.

Miss Sibley was a calm and level-headed person. But even so, well aware there was no means of opening the panel from the inside, she felt an acute lowering of the spirits. For she recalled also that tomorrow was Saturday, when the builders did not come to the house, and that was inevitably followed by Sunday, so that it might be at least fifty hours before anybody became aware of her plight and set her free.

What was she to do in the meantime?

I may as well survey my assets, she thought sensibly, and climbed the stair into the odd-shaped little room above.

The beam of her flashlight, exploring it, showed that the builders had cleared away the dust and left it clean, at least, and bare. There was no indication of anything that might have caused the bangs. Furnishings there were none; Miss Sibley could sit either on the floor or, rather uncomfortably, on one of the crossbeams or joists about a foot above floor level, which meant that she would not be able to raise her head without banging it on the roof behind her.

Oh, well, she thought, at least it is a seat, and she chose the beam, reflecting, with some irony, that she had felt sorry for herself earlier, lying in a comfortable bed, because indigestion prevented her from sleeping; how luxurious, in retrospect, that bed now seemed!

Something scuttled in the corner, and she flinched uncontrollably, catching her breath in what was almost, but not quite, a scream; if there was one thing in the world that filled Miss Sibley with disgust and terror, it was a rat.

"You don't like rats, and yet you're going to live in a mill which must be full of them?" a surprised acquaintance at the bank had inquired, and Miss Sibley had pointed out that the mill had not been working as a mill for at least forty years and had been uninhabited for a further twenty; such rats as there might once have been must surely long since have migrated to more inviting premises and choicer pickings. "I suppose there might be water rats," she said doubtfully, "but they are not nearly so disagreeable, and besides I presume they will stay in the water."

But here, now, was something moving and rustling in that speedy, furtive, stealthy, and, above all, uncontrollable and unpredictable manner so horridly characteristic of rodents; Miss Sibley gave a jump of fright and, doing so, banged her head violently on the roof tiles above.

The pain was severe; she saw stars, and tears flooded her eyes, tears of pain and shock. She gasped out her very worst expletive: *"Oh, blast!"*—and then, somehow, an entirely different deluge of feeling swept over her, different from anything she had ever experienced in her life before, a drenching, mountainous weight of intolerable woe. Like a rock dislodged in a landslip, Miss Sibley toppled to the floor and lay on the boards, with her head pillowed on her arms, drowned in a tidal wave of tears, weeping her heart out.

What for? If asked, she could not possibly have said: for wasted life, for love lost, young years misspent in dusty, unproductive work, for chances mislaid, lapsed friendships, the irretrievable past.

How long she wept she had no notion; hours may have gone by.

But at last, at very long last, like a tiny spark at the

end of an immeasurably long tunnel, came into her head a faint thought: *Yet, after all, here you are, in a mill, as you have always wanted to be, and about to begin making cakes, just as you have always planned?*

That is true, she answered, surprised, and the voice, the thought, which seemed to exist outside, rather than inside her, added, *Perhaps this oddly shaped little room where you find yourself shut up at the moment is like a comma in your life?*

A comma?

A comma, a pause, a break between two thoughts, when you take breath, reconsider, look about, wait for something new to strike you.

Something new.

What in the world am I doing here on the floor, all quenched and draggled, Miss Sibley asked herself, and she raised her head. Unconsciously she had laid her right arm over the joist, and she now noticed, with a frown of surprise, that there was a patch of light on her right wrist, which looked like a luminous watch.

Then, blinking the tears from her eyes, she saw that it was no such thing.

Luminous it *was*, though not very; a faint phosphorescent radiance glimmered from it, similar to that on stale fish, fish that is not all it should be. And two very bright sparks were set close together at one end; and the thing, which was about the size of a bantam's egg, suddenly moved, turning on her wrist, so that the sparks went out and then reappeared in a different place.

Miss Sibley's first violent impulse was to shake her arm, jerk her wrist, rid herself of the thing, whatever it was—bat, vampire, death's-head moth? were some of the wilder notions that flashed into her head.

The second impulse, even more powerful, born of the thought that just a moment before had come to her, was to remain quite still, hold her breath, watch, wait, listen.

She kept still. She waited. She watched the faint luminosity on her wrist.

And she was rewarded.

After a long, quiet, breathing pause, it grew brighter and became recognizable.

Not a rat; definitely not big enough for a rat. But perhaps too large for a common house mouse?

A field mouse?

The thought slipped gently into her head, as had the suggestion about the comma. Wee, sleekit, cowering, something beastie, she thought. Field mice, I've heard, move indoors when autumn winds turn cold; perhaps this one had done that once. It must have been long, long ago, for the mouse was now completely transparent; it had started climbing gently up her arm and the stripes of the cardigan sleeve, red and blue, showed clearly through it.

Of course! Miss Sibley thought. I know who you are! You must be Mr. Watkyn. Dear and charming Watkyn.

A thought like a smile passed across the space between them.

That was Gabriel, yes. He named me. And I, in turn, was able to help him. So we can open doors for one another. When he left—

Yes? When he left?

He left me changed; brought forward, you might say. In this attic here, now, there is still some residue of Gabriel: the pain, the fear; as well as the hope, com-

fort, friendship that we two built between us. Gabriel is buried by now in the churchyard, Watkyn is a pinch of bones and fur long since swallowed by some barn owl; but the product of them lives on and will live as long as hope lives, and hearts to feel hope.

Thank you, Watkyn, said Miss Sibley then; thank you for helping me, and I hope I, too, can help somebody, someday, in the same degree.

Oh, never doubt it, said the voice, closer now, and Miss Sibley lay down to sleep, comfortably, on the flat boards, with Watkyn a faint glimmer of light by her right shoulder.

On Saturday morning Mr. Hoskins visited the mill to pick up a tool he had left there; Mr. Wakehurst, the vicar, had come too, calling, at the same time, to thank Miss Sibley again for the immeasurably valuable gift of the diary; together, with concern, not finding the lady in her kitchen, they searched the house, and she, hearing voices, ran down the little stair and banged on the inside of the panel door until, aghast, they let her out.

"Miss Sibley! What happened?"

"Oh, the door blew closed, in the gale, and shut me in," she said gaily. "You were quite right, Mr. Hoskins; we must change the catch so that can't happen again."

"But you—you are all right? You have been there all night? You were not frightened?" asked the vicar, looking at her searchingly. "Nothing—nothing of an unfortunate nature—occurred?"

"Unfortunate? *No!* Nothing so fortunate has ever happened to me in my whole life!" she told him joyfully, thinking of her future here, decided on, it seemed, so carelessly, in such random haste. And yet what could be more appropriate than to make cakes, to bake beautiful cakes in Hasworth Mill? She would learn the necessary skill, her cakes would grow better and better; and if, at first, a few turned out badly—well, after all, who are more appreciative of cake crumbs than mice?

The Shrieking Door

AFTER FATHER GOT KILLED in an industrial accident, we moved away to live in a wood. Mother didn't want any reminders. We could understand why she did this, in a way, but it was lonely for Alice and me. Lucky we had each other.

Ma got paid some compensation for his death. As if anything *could* compensate, she said, and we agreed. Anyway it wasn't very much. But enough to buy the cottage in the wood (Molloke Copse, part of the New Forest), where Ma was able to support us, more or less, by doing scientific translation from German and reading manuscripts for publishers. Also by renting out rooms. We turned the upstairs part of the cottage into a self-contained flat and advertised in *The Lady*. All summer long there would be people in the flat, coming and going. Mostly they were the quiet kind: people for whom the ad that said, "Secluded, self-contained flat in forest" offered just what they wanted. Professors, painters, and people who wanted to be alone, botanists, musicians, sad people, people who had been ill. Mostly they'd be out all day, riding or driving or walking in the forest. Ma would cook them an evening meal if they wanted, but generally they preferred to take care of themselves.

This arrangement suited Ma very well. She likes solitude, she doesn't want company ("If I'd lived in the Middle Ages, I'd probably have been called a witch," she says), so the odd "good morning" with the lodgers as they passed in and out gave her all she needed.

Alice and I biked to Brockford Halt every day, took the train to Portsbourne, and went to the high school. It was okay. Alice is better at math and music, I'm better at science and art. Neither of us is any use at English. We've no imagination, Mr. Hicks says. We made a few friends, and did the shopping for Ma in Portsbourne after school, and slowly became accustomed to the pain of Father's loss.

At first people took us for twins, as we're very alike. In fact there is a year between us. But Alice, though the older, is more timid than I am. With people, that is. In the forest she is much more confident, being very keen and knowledgeable about wildflowers. She'll go anywhere, miles and miles, to look for a green-man orchid or a broomrape. Whereas—although I love trees individually, I can really have a *relationship* with a tree, I badly missed the old willow tree in the garden of our other house—well, as I say, I can love a tree for itself, but I find a whole mass of them together rather scary. If I'm alone in a wood and a twig snaps, I'm liable to run a mile.

Still, as Alice said, I'd better get over that, for there we were in the middle of a whole forest.

Our cottage, Molloke Cottage, was very old, parts of it went back to Tudor days. The floor was brick, the front door made from one massive oak slab, gray with age. Although it had tiny windows, the house wasn't dark, since it stood in a clearing, quite a big one, where Mother, who enjoys gardening, in a rough-and-ready way, was able to grow vegetables for us and the lodgers, as well as nasturtiums and marigolds. No use trying to grow roses—the deer ate them all. Mr. Hicks told Alice that you can keep away deer if you buy human hair from a barber and tie hanks of it about the garden. We tried doing that, but the deer in our part of the wood seemed immune to the human-hair trick, they went right on coming and ate just as much as ever. At night you could hear them in the garden, munch, munch. Also hedgehogs, which make an amazing noise, like a loud snore; Alice was terrified at first. She thought it was ghosts.

One morning Ma was chuckling over a letter that came in the mail. It cheered us no end to see her laugh; there hadn't been much of that for a long time.

"What is it?" asked Alice.

"A letter from a couple of old biddies who want to come and spend a fortnight in September. I suppose they are nervous elderly spinsters. They say they like the sound of the peace and quiet, but want to know if the house is *haunted*. Well, I can write with a clear conscience and tell them that I've never heard of any such thing."

Alice looked at me, and I looked at her. But neither of us said anything. Why should we, after all? Lodgers had been rather sparse that summer. And Ma would be telling the truth, as far as she knew it. She never gossiped with locals, so she hadn't heard about the shrieking door. And it hadn't shrieked. So that we, who had been told the story by our mates at school, had no particular cause to believe the tale. Our little house was cozy and friendly, smelled of wood smoke and apples when you walked in, accepted squares of sunshine through its tiny windows, and offered no sound apart from the crackle of logs on the fire, or sigh of wind in the chimney. Ma had had new wooden floorboards laid in a couple of rooms, over the bricks, for warmth, and these had shrunk as they dried; just sometimes you'd get that feeling as if somebody else had stepped onto the board you stood on and made it bend a little; that was all. As Mr. Hicks says, Alice and I have no imagination.

So we said nothing to Ma about Squinting Edrica, and Ma wrote and told the two ladies that, to the best of her knowledge, the house was clear of ghost infestation. And in due course the ladies arrived.

They were a slight surprise. For a start, they weren't anything as old as we'd imagined. Both in their late thirties, no more, though Miss Baskin's hair was a soft, beautiful white. Miss Findlater was lean and elegant and dark, with hair upswept in a stylish chignon. She was a sociologist; Miss Baskin taught languages. Each at a different university. That was the second surprise. We had somehow assumed that they lived and spent their lives together. But no, it seemed they only met every five years or so, for a joint holiday. Casual friends, then? Yet we did get the feeling they were very, very devoted to one another. Even from odd glimpses, as they ran down the stairs and out into the forest or came back, grass-stained, holding bunches of berries and scabious, at the end of the day, it was possible to see what a lot they meant to each other. Although Miss Baskin's name was Gloria, and Miss Findlater's Olive, they addressed each other gaily as "B" or "my B"; I had just been reading a book about the Ladies of Llangollen and knew this was an abbreviation for "my beloved."

Another thing that struck us as a little odd was that Miss Findlater brought along with her a canary in a cage and a goldfish in a bowl; but, she explained, reasonably enough, there was nobody she could ask to look after them in her block of flats. And she kept them upstairs; they were no trouble.

Ma took quite a liking to the Ladies (as we soon began to call them) and chatted with them more than was her custom as they passed back and forth. When Miss Findlater was laid up one day with a cold, she invited Miss Baskin to share our Sunday dinner. The Ladies were her kind of people, she said; they were interesting, did things, read things, knew things.

One point did puzzle her, and so, being a blunt, forthright character, she came out with it while Miss Baskin was eating roast lamb and gooseberry tart in our kitchen.

If you don't ask, you don't learn, is one of Mother's favorite maxims.

"You and Miss Findlater seem such close friends," she said, "I don't understand why you see one another so infrequently. The last time was four years ago, you said? That seems so odd to me. I mean, these days . . ."

Miss Baskin frowned, smiled, tapped her fingers on the blue and white cloth.

"It must seem perverse, I know," she said. "When we are, as you say, so fond of one another. We've known each other all our lives; we were at school together. But—well—this *thing* gradually grew up, and it leads to such trouble—"

She gave a doubtful glance in the direction of Alice

and me, but Mother said, "Oh, the girls are used to anything. They've seen me through their father's death; they are very adult for their age. They really know all there is to know."

About things like lesbianism, was what she plainly meant, but Miss Baskin said, "To tell you the truth, when we heard there were two teenage girls in the house, we nearly changed our minds."

As we looked, I suppose, particularly blank, she went on: "Poltergeist manifestations, you know, are almost invariably associated with the presence of pubertal young people. But your two seem particularly well balanced and sensible."

"*Poltergeists?*" said Mother. "I don't quite understand?"

"Well—you see—" Miss Baskin looked a little embarrassed. "It sounds almost unbelievably silly, but it isn't. It can be quite serious—even tragic. Separate from each other, Olive and I are just two ordinary people, as commonplace as can be. But when we are together, we seem to have some queer catalytic effect on our surroundings. If there *is* any kind of supernatural manifestation about, the pair of us together may call it up. Once, when we were much younger, we went to Spain together and stayed at a government-run hotel that had been a monastery in the Middle Ages. My goodness, the thought of what happened there still makes me shake. And in other hotels, schools, colleges, people's homes— well, as I say, we've practically given up meeting. But we are so fond of each other that it really is a great deprivation for both of us. So, once in a while, if we can find some small, quiet, out-of-the-way spot, we chance it."

I didn't dare look toward Alice. I knew, because of

the close bond between us, what she must be feeling—guilt, fright, anger, and a kind of depression. Why should Mother's chance of earning a few extra pounds have to depend on our keeping quiet about Squinting Edrica and her door? We might just as easily *not* have heard the story; in fact it is the kind of thing that is generally concealed from prospective house buyers.

Squinting Edrica lived some time in the sixteenth century. She was a wealthy farmer's daughter. She never married because of her bad squint; crossed eyes were thought unlucky then, a result of having been overlooked by the Evil One. So, although otherwise quite handsome, Edrica remained a spinster, and when her father died, despite the fact that she was his eldest daughter, her younger brother inherited the property, because the farmhands wouldn't have worked for a woman, let alone a cross-eyed one. Her brother gave her a decent allowance and built her this cottage in the wood. And, of course, by and by, she was assumed to be a witch; that was inevitable, because of her looks, and her solitary life. It was said that she used to go and talk to a huge tree, the Moll Oak, that stood on the boundary between two parishes. People said she lit Satan's fire under it and danced with fiends. So a posse of do-gooders went out with saws and hatchets and cut down the oak. If the truth be known, they probably had a good use for the timber. Edrica had an ally in the village, a man whose child she had cured of the wasting sickness with a tincture of moly, or sorcerer's garlic. This man managed to smuggle her a big plank from the felled oak and made her a door out of it. And, unlike other witches, who have a bird or a cat as her familiar demon, Edrica was supposed to use the door itself, put questions to it, tell it all the news, and, in return, the door would warn her if enemies were approaching by letting out a loud shriek. So, several times, when hostile villagers came to her cottage with the aim of putting her in the stocks or ducking her in the horse pond, the door warned her beforehand by shrieking, and she hid far away in the forest until they grew tired of waiting and went home. Sometimes they broke her furniture or threw her pots about, but she lived very simply, with few possessions, and had precious little they could harm. Perhaps her brother the farmer would help replace what was broken; he must have felt a bit of guilt about her being passed over when he inherited the property.

But in the end the neighbors got the better of Edrica. They arrived when she was tired, after sitting up two nights with a woman in labor; they brought moonwort, which has the property of unlocking locks and unshoeing horses and undoing the effects of spells; they also brought holy water, and drenched the door with that, so that it could not shriek; using these means, they were able to break into the house. Edrica was tied up and dragged off to a huge pile of branches in a clearing, where she was duly burned. And the door, it was said, wailed and cried like a child all the time this was going on, and everybody who had touched the door died within a year.

"You'd think they'd have burned the door too," said Alice skeptically when someone told her the story.

"Perhaps they didn't like to waste such a fine slab of wood," I suggested.

"I expect the truth is that the story grew up years after. They'd have burned the door fast enough if they really believed it belonged to the devil. What awful lives women had then."

"Are they so much better now?" I wondered.

"Much better," Alice said stoutly.

I remembered that conversation when Miss Baskin told us about herself and her friend. They seemed such a quiet, sympathetic, affectionate pair; it was terrible bad luck on them that they had this peculiar power. Probably they would far rather not have had it. And I wondered, in a vague way, whether the power had sprung up *because* they were obliged to live apart; supposing they had always been together, comfortably, might it never have arisen?

The intensity of longing for someone who isn't with you can be very bad, I knew. Mother, Alice, and I all longed for Father in our different ways. Alice went off into the forest and had long spells of crying, from which she would return silent, subdued, and red-eyed. Mother could sometimes be heard walking to and fro, to and fro, in her bedroom well into the small hours. I felt, all the time, a dreadful inner ache, like a hunger that nothing could appease. Perhaps Edrica, too, had felt something like this? Perhaps she had loved some person who wouldn't look at her, because of the squint; perhaps she felt just such a hopeless pain when she passed his house or saw him ride by on a horse?

Maybe that power of feeling, hidden away, suppressed, had been somehow transmuted, sublimated, into the power to cure warts (if that was what Edrica did) or summon up poltergeists?

Miss Findlater's cold got better, and the Ladies resumed their habit of going out for day-long excursions. Ma often made them up a packed lunch.

One thing she would *not* do was have the canary and the goldfish downstairs while they were out.

"It was only a suggestion," Miss Findlater said apologetically. "They do so enjoy human company. And they get so little of it at home, as I'm out all day teaching."

But Mother was firm.

"I don't like the company of things in cages," she said.

"I quite agree with you," remarked Miss Baskin.

This was, we gathered, a point on which the Ladies were not in perfect accord. From time to time we'd hear Gloria teasing her friend in a tone that lacked its usual friendliness, was verging on sharp, in fact.

"How can you bear to have those two poor prisoners always about? Why don't you set them free?"

And Olive would reply, not in her normal, gentle tones but quite snappishly, "Oh, please don't be so silly, Gloria! How can you set a goldfish free, pray? Or a canary? What am I supposed to do? Let it fly off into the forest? A fine time it would have there! I can just imagine what kind of a short, nasty life my poor Billy-bird would have in the forest!"

"Well, you shouldn't encourage the trade by getting them in the first place."

"The trade will go on, with or without my support. And I must have *some* company."

I must say, they seemed poor sort of company to me: a twittering, fluttering nervous bird and a mute fish that did nothing but swim around and around. However, it was not my business; on the whole we liked the Ladies very well.

We did notice, though, that, as their visit went on, they seemed to bicker and disagree more and more often.

Matters came to a head one afternoon when a

heavy shower had driven them in much earlier than usual. They stopped for a cup of tea in our kitchen.

Mother was lamenting about the habits of the deer, which had munched up a whole row of young beans.

"Wretched things! There's just no way to keep them out."

"We need some new hair," I suggested.

"*Hair!* What does hair do?"

The Ladies had never heard the theory about human hair as a deer deterrent and were eager to try it out.

"We'll cut each other's hair—we can both spare a bit, and we often used to do each other's when we were younger. We'll see if that has any effect."

Giggling like schoolgirls, they borrowed Mother's sharp scissors and a pile of towels, then set to work on each other in the kitchen.

But the results were unfortunate. Perhaps they had lost their skill since those young days. Or become more particular. They didn't look too bad to me and Alice, but neither of them was a bit pleased with what the other had done.

"You didn't have to chop off *quite* so much!" exclaimed Gloria. "I can't pin it up at the back now. It's all wispy."

"You've taken off the part that curls! I look like Mad Maggie!" wailed Olive, looking at herself in the glass over the sink. "What *will* my students say?"

Mother tried to make peace by giving them slices of a sponge cake she had baked, and Alice did her best to throw oil on troubled waters by exclaiming over the panful of black and white hair as she swept it up, "It's so *beautiful*! Like magic stuff! I'm sure it will keep the deer off the late peas. There's such a lot, I'll be able to sprinkle it all along the row."

Unfortunately even the beauty of the chopped-off black and white hair had no effect; next morning there were deer tracks all over the bed, and most of the peas were gone.

"And we lost our hair for nothing!" growled Miss Baskin. "What you ought to have, Mrs. Kirby, is a trap. Then you could have venison for supper."

"A trap!" Miss Findlater's voice was full of horror and disgust. "How can you make such a heartless suggestion? You, the one who calls herself fond of animals! You, who wants me to get rid of my poor Billy-bird! And who would kill the deer, pray, as it lay in the garden with its leg in the trap? Do you expect Mrs. Kirby to go out with a chopper? Or one of the girls to wring its neck?"

"All right, all right! I was only joking."

"A fine sort of joke."

Very ill pleased with each other, the friends set off on their usual excursion.

While they wrangled, I had been aware of an odd noise, an unfamiliar noise that I could not place. But when they had started Miss Findlater's little car and driven off into the forest, I was able to locate the sound. It came from our front door.

The day was glum and damp, oppressively close in spite of the fact that a small, fidgety wind was stirring the trees, making the branches creak. But the wind hardly seemed sufficient to fetch such a wail from the door. It was like a suppressed moan, from a person in unbearable pain: "Oh—oh!" And again: "Oh—oh!"

"For heaven's sake!" said Mother. "The door's never made that sound before. We'd better oil the hinges."

It was a Saturday, no school for Alice and me, so

we helped Ma do this; but oil made no difference. At intervals every twenty minutes or so, the door would suddenly let out its grievous, keening note.

Around lunchtime Mother said: "I don't know if it's because of the door or what, but I've suddenly got the most atrocious headache. I'll have to lie down for a while."

Of course we said don't worry, and we'd do the housework and washing that was usually done on Saturdays. But after an hour Alice went up to Ma with a cup of tea and came back looking pale and anxious.

"I think she's really ill. I think we'd better phone the doctor."

Of course, it being Saturday, he was out playing golf. When we finally got him (I did the telephoning because Alice can't stand phones or dealing with people), he sounded really concerned.

"You say she keeps on letting out little shrieks and hardly knows you? I think you'd better get her to a hospital right away. The ambulance is over at Chetwood, where there's been a bad road smash, and I'm here at the club ten miles off—every minute may make a difference—can you drive her?"

"Yes," I said.

"Then get her in the car and take her straight to Portsbourne Hospital and I'll meet you there."

"All right," I said, my knees knocking together.

I *can* drive, actually, because I've practiced on tracks in the forest. But I'm too young, at sixteen, legally to be in charge of a car on the road. And Alice, who passed her test, is so sick with terror at the wheel that no one in their senses would go in a car driven by her.

So Alice sat in the back, her arms around Mother,

while I drove, with adrenaline prickling up and down my arms, a hollow stomach, a stiff back, and a mouth dry with fear. Mercifully the hospital, a big new one, is on the outskirts of Portsbourne; I'd never have had the courage to go through the town.

Dr. Mayor met us as promised, took one look at Mother, and whizzed her to the intensive care unit. He later told us that what she had was something-ococcal meningitis, and that it was a good thing we'd brought her in fast, for she would be all right now, but she might easily not have been.

We had to have tests, too, which took some time, and he told us that it would be no use our going to see Mother today, as she was under heavy sedation; we could come back tomorrow.

Then because, I suppose, we both looked wan and shaky and exhausted, he said we'd better not drive ourselves home; and he found a young male nurse going off duty who lived in our general direction and would tie his motorbike to the rack on top of our car and drive us. We were very grateful to this character (his name was Fred)—even more so when we got home and, at our approach, the front door let out a wild scream.

"Glory hallelujah, what's *that*?" said Fred, startled out of his wits.

"Oh—it's our door. It does that sometimes," mumbled Alice.

"Not too often, I hope!"

As we opened the front door, Miss Findlater came running down the stairs.

Her white hair was wildly untidy, her face pale and distraught.

"Have you seen Gloria?" she demanded, without apparently noticing that Mother was missing or that we had arrived, late and worried, in the company of a strange young man.

"No, we just got back from taking Mother to the hospital—haven't you been together?"

"No, we had a qua—we had words, and went off separately. But Gloria must have been back because— because—because—she opened the cage! My Billy-bird is missing! And the fish—she must have emptied it into the brook—she was threatening to, but I never believed she would really do such a cruel thing—"

At this gabble Alice and I looked at each other, aghast. Miss Findlater sounded half demented—and it sounded as if the composed, elegant Miss Baskin must have had some kind of brainstorm too.

"Help me look for her?" begged Miss Findlater. "Oh, I'll have to give her such a talking-to when I find her! She must have gone out of her mind!"

"Yes, we'll help," Alice said wearily. For what else could we do? "But you must—you must be gentle with her when you see her. It sounds as if she must be ill— must need a doctor."

Fred, who plainly had a very kind nature, said he would stop and help us search for Miss Baskin.

We managed to persuade Miss Findlater, who looked desperately tired and shattered—she had gone quite cross-eyed with distress—to stay in the house, in case her friend came back. "Keep the fire up in the kitchen stove," Alice recommended. "And make us some hot soup."

And the three of us went off into the forest in different directions, calling and shouting, "Miss Baskin! Miss Baskin! Glo—o—oria!"

Twilight was falling, and I've never felt so nervous and jumpy in the forest. Every snap of a twig made me gasp and clench my teeth. The branches creaked overhead, and the wind sighed and blubbered.

I was the one who eventually found Miss Baskin.

She was sitting on a huge tree stump, moaning and rocking back and forth, her head bowed and her arms around her knees.

I was really terrified when I first saw her, because it was almost dark by then, and in the half-light she hardly seemed human, more like some shapeless wild beast. It took a really strong effort to go up and touch her hand.

"Miss Baskin! Miss Baskin! You must come back to the house, your friend is very worried about you."

Then she looked up at me. In the dusk her face, with its dark tangled hair about it, was white as a bowl of junket.

"I did an unkind thing, a wicked thing. I let go her creatures. I couldn't stand the sight of them any longer."

"Well, she'll have to get over it," I said. "She can buy others, can't she? But you must come back now, she's worried to death about you."

"Yes, yes," she muttered. "I must come back, I must come back."

And suddenly, without waiting for me, she jumped up and dashed off headlong in the direction of our cottage.

I followed as fast as I could, but I could not keep up her pace. It had been a long, awful day. I was really tired by now. Miss Baskin fled away in front of me, shouting, "Olive! Olive! I'm coming, I'm coming, wait for me!" in a childish, whimpering voice. I followed, panting and gulping, catching my feet in holes and under fallen boughs, while my jeans and shirt were snagged and dragged by gorse and brambles. The forest had never seemed more dark and hostile.

Yet there was a light ahead. What could it be? No light was ever seen in that part of the wood, except the small, dim gleam from our cottage's tiny windows. But this light was blazing and fierce, buttercup yellow and leaping. . . .

When I reached our garden glade, I saw why. The cottage was on fire, and burning like a paper bag. Flames, curved and plaited, shot twenty feet into the sky. A roar filled the air—and yet through it all I thought I could hear the satisfied shriek of the front door, its debt paid at last.

"Olive!" shouted Miss Baskin again. "Olive! *Wait for me, Olive!*" and without a second's hesitation she dashed headlong into the flames.

Cousin Alice

WHEN FERN ROBSON went to stay with her
mother's sister, her aunt Twyla, it was out of acute
need, not for any pleasant reason.

"She's an awkward one, Twyla Deane," sighed Mr.
Robson. "There's no denying that. But where else to
send you I just do not know."

Mrs. Robson, Fern's mother, had been very badly
injured in an excursion bus accident on a day's outing
to Paigle Bay, and it was not even certain yet whether
she would recover. She was in intensive care, in a deep
coma. And her husband, Sam, with a broken leg, was
hobbling about in a nearby ward, not allowed out of the
hospital, though he was well enough to make arrangements about his daughter.

"You'll just have to go to Twyla, dearie. I'm right
sorry about it, but there it is."

Fern was sorry too. Apart from the dreadful non-
stop pain and fear about her mother, she hated leaving
home, because the month was May, and the sweet peas
were coming up in her garden patch, and the lilacs in

front of the cottage, and the bluebells in Slype Wood down the lane. Who'd want to go and stay on the edge of a growing town, in a house by the railway?

"Who'll feed Smokey while I'm away?"

"The neighbors. He'll manage. You be a good girl, now, and don't argue."

So Fern miserably packed a bag, and Tom Harman, one of the neighbors, drove her thirty miles to Haleswick and left her at Aunt Twyla's house.

Crossing Cottage, the place was called, because of the level crossing nearby. It was not a cottage really, but a bungalow, built of ugly raw red brick with a slate roof. The garden was flat and bare, not a tree in it, only some empty-looking flower beds alternating with concrete paths and poor-looking grass. There wasn't a tree to be seen *anywhere*, in fact; close by lay timber yards and goods yards and factory sheds, a bit of wasteland with junk cars and nettles, the railway, of course, and, right on the other side of Aunt Twyla's garden fence, an enormous electric pylon, towering over the squat little house, its four legs planted so far apart that the square of ground between them seemed bigger than the garden itself. There were half a dozen notices fixed on the pylon: DANGER, KEEP AWAY, HIGH VOLTAGE, BEWARE, PROPERTY of the ELECTRICITY BOARD, TRESPASSERS WILL BE PROSECUTED.

Since almost the first thing Aunt Twyla told Fern was that she would be frizzled up like a thread in a flame if she ever touched the pylon, TRESPASSERS WILL BE PROSECUTED hardly seemed necessary, Fern thought. There wouldn't be much left of them to prosecute.

The pylon hummed to itself now and then, a feverish mosquito sound that Fern didn't care for at all. While the hum went on, she found it hard to concentrate on her school work, hard to fall asleep at night, hard to do anything but worry about how Mother was getting on.

The other children at the Haleswick school were standoffish at first.

"Your aunt, Mrs. Deane, is a queer one," they told Fern. "That's why her old man goes to sea; he goes to sea because he can't stand her."

"He goes to sea because he's a merchant seaman," said Fern reasonably. "He comes back every six months."

"He don't stay home long. She quarrels with folk, your aunt does. Where she lived before, she quarreled with the neighbors so bad, she had to move."

This was true, Fern discovered, or partly true. For years the Deanes had lived in the High Street, in a small, ancient gabled house, next to a greengrocer's shop. But there had been trouble. What sort of trouble Fern could not make out, but anyway, while Uncle Frank was off at sea, Aunt Twyla had left the house in which her husband had been born and moved to Crossing Cottage.

"No neighbors to fret me here," she said tersely. "It's better."

Aunt Twyla was a terse woman, silent, thin, and angry-faced, only uttering when she had to; twelve hours a day she wore an apron and had her hair scraped back as if she didn't care what it looked like.

It was a pity about the house in the High Street, Fern thought. It had bow windows and was built of stone, looked solid and comfortable; next door to it the greengrocer's always had beautiful high-piled fragrant masses of pinks and roses and lilies-of-the-valley, besides lettuce and onions and cauliflowers and fruit. Flowers and vegetables next door would be much more comfortable than the pylon and the railway; all through each night trains clanked and shunted and whimpered and flung electric flashes over Fern's bedroom ceiling. Aunt Twyla's curtains were thin cotton; the light flashed through.

"Don't the trains ever keep you awake?" Fern asked.

But Aunt Twyla said, "I never do sleep much."

"Mother doesn't either."

"I know," said Twyla. Then she added slowly, "Maybe she's making up for that now."

Fern remembered her mother saying once, "Twyla and I used to have the same dreams. At breakfast we used to check with each other about the bits we couldn't remember. I wonder if we still dream the same things?"

What was Mother dreaming now? Fern wondered; and then, looking at Aunt Twyla, thought, Is that what she is wondering too?

The bungalow was small and bare and flimsy. Even with only two people there, it was hard to get off and be alone, because every corner seemed visible from every other corner. Unless you went into the bathroom. There were no books or pictures, and the floor was bare polished linoleum.

No photographs. Fern had wondered if there would be one of Alice, but there was not. Nor of Uncle Frank.

"Whatever you do, don't mention Alice," Father had warned, and Fern had promised she would not.

Alice was her cousin, Aunt Twyla's daughter, who had died in an accident seven years ago. Fern had been only three when Alice died, the same age as her cousin. Of course there wouldn't be any clothes or toys left. Aunt Twyla would have got rid of them long ago. It was

all over. And had happened when the Deanes were living in the other house, the one in the High Street.

Fern used to pass the house every day as she went
to and from school. She used to look up at the windows
and wonder which one had been Alice's room.

Living in a house without any upstairs was queer,
and not comfortable. Fern often found herself, in Crossing Cottage, absentmindedly listening for the sound of
footsteps overhead, and almost sure that she heard
them. Or footsteps coming down the stairs. She never
could get used to the fact that there weren't any stairs.

Nobody lived in the High Street house now; it had
been turned into estate agents' offices. There were no
lights in the window at night.

Coming home late sometimes, from Girl Scouts or
a school film show, Fern would look up at the dark
windows and think, Suppose Alice is still there? Not
very nice for her, all alone in a dark, empty house full of
photographs of houses. And she sent a thought through
the black, empty glass of the windows: Cousin Alice?
Are you there? I'm sorry we never met. It wouldn't be
so miserable, staying in Crossing Cottage, if *you* were
there too.

June the first was Mother's birthday. Fern sent a greet-
ings telegram to the hospital: THINKING ABOUT YOU ALL THE
TIME LOVE FERN. And Aunt Twyla rang up Father, who
was still in the hospital, too; his leg wasn't mending as
fast as it should. He said there was no change in
Mother's condition. Still in a coma.

Fern went to school as usual, feeling as if lead
weights were tied on her feet. Coming home at teatime,
past Coney's vegetable and flower shop, she was re-
minded by the colorful, fragrant display that if it was

Mother's birthday, it must be Aunt Twyla's birthday, too, since they were twins, so she stopped and bought a bunch of pinks. They were pink and white and frilly and smelt powerfully sweet, of clove and vanilla.

"You are Mrs. Deane's niece, aren't you?" said Mrs. Coney, plump and gray-haired, wrapping a twist of tissue paper around the pinks. "Wasn't your mother in an accident? How is she getting on?"

The concern and kindness in her voice nearly undid Fern, who had managed all through the schoolday to wear a crust of calm. Her lip began to quiver; she muttered, "N-not too well," and almost bolted out of the shop.

She didn't stop, as usual, to send a thought up to Cousin Alice next door, but hurried homeward, out of the cheerful High Street, into Gasworks Road, along Brewery Way, through Salt Passage, and so to Railway Approach and the flimsy iron gate of Crossing Cottage.

There had been rain during the afternoon; the cracked, unmade-up footway of Railway Approach was muddy and puddly. Aunt Twyla detested wet feet making marks on the clean linoleum floor, and even through her fog of misery about Mother, Fern managed to remember that; she took pains to avoid the puddles and reached the garden gate with dry feet. The sloping concrete path to the front door had already dried off, but as Fern walked up it, she noticed a line of wet footprints ahead of her. Some other person evidently had *not* troubled to avoid the puddles. Some other person had feet about the same size as Fern's own. Who could it be?

Nobody—and especially not children—ever came calling at Crossing Cottage. Twyla's only visitors were men coming to read the meter and ladies selling flags in aid of cancer research.

Fern opened the door and nearly fell over her aunt, who was ironing pillow slips. There wasn't room to do more than one thing at a time in the bungalow—with the ironing board unfolded you had to squeeze along the wall.

Fern put down her schoolbag and looked around the room, which was bare and tidy. No visitor, nothing unusual.

"Is anyone here?" she couldn't help asking.

"*I'm* here. Nobody else," snapped her aunt. "Why?"

Fern was embarrassed. She was afraid Aunt Twyla might think she had expected to find a birthday party in process—which she certainly had not.

"It's just—I thought I saw—" she mumbled, and turned to look through the open front door behind her. But the line of wet footprints had dried off the path; there was nothing to be seen.

"Shut that door, such a perishing draft it makes when the back door's open," said Aunt Twyla sharply. The front and back doors were directly opposite each other, with the scullery, front room, and a bit of passage between. If all the doors happened to be open, in whatever direction the wind was blowing, it seemed to veer around and sweep through the house.

"I bought these for you, Aunt Twyla," said Fern. "Happy birthday!" And she handed her aunt the bunch of pinks.

Aunt Twyla's eyes sparked as she turned back the tissue. "Where did you get these?" she demanded.

"Coney's, in the High Street."

"I don't want you getting things there, ever. D'you hear?"

"Why, Aunt Twyla?"

"Because I say so. I don't want you having anything to do with those Coneys. Just remember that."

Aunt Twyla walked quickly away with the pinks. She certainly did not put them into a vase. After tea, wondering what had happened to them, Fern went out into the glum little back garden, with its rotary clothes dryer, ash heap, dustbin, and empty rabbit hutch left over from the previous owner. On the other side of the fence the pylon hummed menacingly. At first Fern couldn't see the pinks, on the ash heap or anywhere about the garden, but then she noticed them lying under the pylon, midway between its four massive steel feet. Aunt Twyla must have flung them there, over the fence. They were light; she must have flung them with all her strength.

That evening, unusually, Twyla went out and left Fern alone in the bungalow. Where had Aunt Twyla gone? Was she walking fast, angrily, through the draggled fields, past the gasworks and the sewage farm? Fern lay shivering in bed, listening to the hum of the pylon and the howl of passing trains.

Next day at school Sue Coney, who was fat and curly-headed and good-natured, and had, up to now, been rather a friend of Fern's, wrote her a note that said, "After what your aunt did, I don't want to be friends anymore."

Fern hated mysteries. She went up to Sue Coney at break time—Sue was in the class below hers—and said, "What is this about? I don't understand. What did my aunt do?"

"She knocked over our posy tubs," said Sue Coney.

On each side of the greengrocer's shop there were two big ornamental tubs standing out on the pavement, filled with growing flowers, tulips or marigolds or lobelias, whatever was in season.

Fern had noticed, on the way to school, that the tubs had been pushed over; earth and dying plants lay scattered all over the sidewalk. Perhaps a car had skidded and upset the tubs, Fern thought at the time.

But Sue said, "Your aunt did it."

"How do you know?"

"Dad says so."

"I don't believe it. Why should she do a thing like that?"

"Dad says it must have been her."

"Why?"

"Because of what she did before." And Sue went off to the other side of the playground.

Another girl, Tessa Leigh, explained. "There used to be a lot of trouble between your aunt and the Coneys. That was why she moved to Crossing Cottage. There was always bad feeling over one thing or another. She complained they made too much noise—their dog bit her cat, or t'other way around—Oz Coney chopped some branches off a tree in the hedge between the gardens that Mrs. Deane said was her tree—there was a row about repairs to an inside wall—they couldn't ever be friendly about anything. Of course really it all went back to little Alice."

"*What* about little Alice?" asked Fern, wondering why she found it so hard to breathe.

"That was the kid that died. Mrs. Deane's little girl. She was out playing one day in the back garden— they have nice big gardens behind those houses in the

High Street—she scrambled through a gap in the hedge and went into the Coneys' garden."

"Well?"

"That was it. They had a well, a deep one. It's all filled in now; they turned it into a little garden pond, with plants and goldfish. There's a spring, you see. But in those times it was eighty feet deep, with a bucket and winding handle. Folks said it was a wishing well. They still do, as a matter of fact."

"What happened?"

"The kid fell down the well. Wasn't found till it was too late."

"How awful. Oh, how awful."

"Your aunt blamed the Coneys. Said the well should have been covered over. Said other things too—" Tessa stopped short.

How could she bear it? thought Fern. No wonder she had never been on friendly terms with the Coney family since. Though they weren't really to blame. . . .

But still—to upset their tubs and throw the flowers in the road—*could* Aunt Twyla really have done a spiteful thing like that?

"I don't believe Aunt Twyla did it," Fern said to Sue Coney after school, and Sue said, "Well, Dad thinks she did. He's furious. He's going to arrange the Railway Walk. He said if it weren't for that, he wouldn't have bothered; he was going to have let it lapse this year. But now he's going to make sure they do it."

"What on earth is the Railway Walk?"

"Your aunt bought that bungalow in a hurry from old Fred Stoppard. He was the one who built it. When he built it, he didn't know, and he didn't tell your aunt when he sold it to her, that there's a right of way clean through the house."

"What does that mean?" asked Fern.

"It's like a public footpath going right through. Any person has the right to walk in at your aunt's front door and out at the back, and on through that gate in the right-hand fence, along the path that goes in a tunnel under the railway and out to the river and the sewage farm. I've heard that your uncle nearly had a fit when he came back from the sea and found what she'd got instead of his old house in the High Street."

"But," said Fern, puzzled, "nobody *does* walk through my aunt's house."

"No, they don't, because people are a bit scared of her. Some of them even think she's a witch. Anyway, there's plenty of other ways to get to the sewage farm. But if there's a right of way, you're supposed to make sure it's walked along, at least once a year, and that's what Dad's always done. He's on the town council in charge of footpaths, you see. Your aunt gets riled when they come and do it, but they're allowed; she can't stop them. The councillors bring their wives and people from the Haleswick Historical and any ratepayers who want to come. They're going to do it the day after tomorrow, Sunday."

"Well, *I* think it's hateful," burst out Fern. "Especially—"

Especially when Mother's so ill, perhaps dying, she thought, but she could see that was beside the point.

"Your aunt shouldn't have knocked over those tubs of flowers."

"Nobody saw her. No one can prove she did. And anyway I'm sure she didn't."

When Fern got home that evening, Aunt Twyla was very pale, even more silent than usual, and her mouth was set in a bitter line. A letter headed Haleswick Urban District Council stood on the mantelpiece; she did not say anything about it to Fern, who had her own matter for silent thought: The line of wet footprints had been there again, ahead of her on the path as she walked up to the house. She had seen them appearing, one by one, all the way to the door.

Who had stepped through the doorway just ahead of her?

Later, as she sat trying to do her homework on the kitchen table, when the hum of the pylon died down, she felt certain that she could hear somebody moving about upstairs—opening a drawer, maybe, taking a book off a shelf or a toy from a cupboard.

But there wasn't any upstairs in the bungalow.

On Sunday morning Fern, feeling rather sick, said, "I think I'll go out for a walk." But Aunt Twyla said, "No. You stay right here." So Fern stayed. Her mouth was dry, it was like the first day at school, only much worse.

At eleven they all arrived, quite a large group of people, wearing dark, respectable clothes as if they were going to a funeral or a court case. A few carried umbrellas, because it was raining a bit. They didn't knock at the door or ring the doorbell, but walked straight in, led by Mr. Coney, a tall man with light gray fluffy hair and very blue eyes like his daughter. Some of the people looked embarrassed, but he didn't; he was just very serious.

"Come for the right-of-way walk, Mrs. Deane," he said.

Aunt Twyla made no answer. She was ironing curtains and had arranged her board across the room so that there was only just enough space to edge around it.

Mr. Coney made as if to lift the ironing board. Then Aunt Twyla did speak.

"You'd better not touch that!" she said, "or I'll have the law on you!"

So Mr. Coney and the rest of his twenty-nine companions had to edge carefully around the side of the ironing board, step gingerly over the cord of the iron, and so through the passage, the scullery, the back door, and across the garden to the side gate that led into the lane.

"Thank you, Mrs. Deane," each person said politely as he or she left.

Twyla waited until the last was out, Dr. Leigh; then she went into the garden. The group were still in the lane, writing on their clipboards. Aunt Twyla said—and the words seemed to come out of her like water under fierce pressure—

"You have left filthy footprints all over my clean linoleum. You know what I think of you? I think you are *vermin*. You deserve every bit of bad luck that will come to you. And it can't be worse than I wish it."

Then she turned on her heel and went back into the house.

Next day at school Fern came in for a good many cold looks. She felt this was rather hard; she was not responsible for the feud between Aunt Twyla and the Coneys, or for any part of what had happened; except, true, that she had bought that unlucky bunch of pinks.

Matters were made worse because Sue Coney, that very day, had suddenly come down with what Dr. Leigh called a particularly tricky kind of virus pneumonia, and her parents were worried to death about her. No one spoke out directly, or said this was a result of Aunt Twyla's ill-wishing, but some people really thought it, and things were muttered behind hands, especially among the children at school.

Fat Ozzie Coney, Sue's retarded elder brother, who was eighteen, and worked in the brick factory, lurched threateningly up to Fern after school and growled at her, "You'd better tell your aunt to take that thing off."

"What thing?" said Fern, puzzled.

"That thing she laid on our Sue! Else we'll make this place too hot to hold her."

And Ozzie giggled suddenly, as he was liable to do in the middle of any conversation, whether funny or not, and rolled his eyes sideways at Fern, and shambled away.

"Don't take too much notice of him," said Tessa. "He's always been like that."

In the evening, when Fern went home, she found Aunt Twyla grimly sticking elastic plaster over several holes in the front windows where stones had been thrown. A policeman was there inspecting the damage. He shook his head, said it was no doubt boys at their pranks, and that unfortunately the police force was short staffed and couldn't possibly keep an eye on Crossing Cottage at all hours of the day and night, but of course they'd do their best.

He did not sound as if he himself intended to do his best.

Next day, though, there was a sudden, unexpected change. People at school were friendly again, and Mrs. Coney, outside her shop arranging bunches of radishes, made a point of stopping Fern, as she walked home with Tessa, to say they were all very sorry for misjudging her aunt over those flower tubs, but mistakes did get made sometimes, and she hoped Mrs. Deane wouldn't have any hard feelings, and how was Fern's mother? She asked as if she really wanted to know, but Fern could only reply that her mother was still much the same.

"Oh, dear, that's too bad." Mrs. Coney sounded honestly sorry.

"Father says we need a miracle," Fern muttered. "What about Sue, Mrs. Coney?"

Mrs. Coney's good-natured face looked suddenly haggard.

"She's poorly. She's very poorly. If miracles are being given out, we could use one too." And she walked slowly inside, past the boxes of oranges.

"You'd think," said Tessa Leigh, "that she'd wish on her wishing well."

"Wishing well—? Oh! In the garden. But it doesn't really work, does it?"

"Of course it works!" said Tessa, rather indignantly. "I've wished for lots of things when I went to tea with Sue and always got them. A pair of green sandals—and a fine day on my birthday—and to be top in math—"

"You can't prove—"

"Can't prove? Who needs to? I know!"

Perhaps you need to believe in it, Fern thought, and Mrs. Coney doesn't. But I would. Oh, I think I'd believe.

She turned back and went into the shop.

"Mrs. Coney—might I have a wish on your wishing well?"

Mrs. Coney was serving a customer with four pounds of potatoes, a melon, and some rhubarb. She said absently, "Of course, love. Help yourself. Down the path at the side and through the green gate."

She was wrapping up the rhubarb in newspaper.

Fern read the headline on it: BOYS OWN UP TO HIGH STREET VANDALISM.

"Shocking, isn't it, the things those young tearaways get up to? Lucky Sergeant Ferson caught them at it," the customer said.

Fern ran down the little snicket path beside the Coneys' house, through the green gate, and made her way to the end of the narrow, quiet garden. There was a pear tree, and a quince tree, a patch of bright green mossy lawn, and a forsythia, just shedding its yellow petals and beginning to put out new green leaves. The pool was under the pear tree, ringed by spears of iris, and with drifted white pear blossoms floating in its dark green water.

Fern knelt on the brick paving at the edge and looked in. She could see her own reflection, sliced neatly in two by a goldfish that swam across. The reflection looked much younger than she felt.

She put her hand into the cold water. I ought to drop something in, she thought. I haven't any money. What do I have in my schoolbag that would do? And remembered her ivory penknife that Granny Sands had given her. It had been Granny's and Great-granny's; it had a large blade and a small, and she loved it dearly.

In it went.

"Mother," whispered Fern. "Oh, *Mother* . . . Sue . . ." and then, for some reason, she was hardly sure why, she whispered, "Alice . . . Cousin Alice," and went on crouching in silence for a while, staring down into the murky water; until a fish jumped for a fly, with a sudden plop, and startled her.

She was late coming home, and Aunt Twyla was cross.

"Wondering where you'd got to," she snapped.

"That Oz Coney's been around, mumbling and muttering and acting peculiar. I don't like his looks. Never have—" and then she bit off something she might have been going to say and slapped a pair of plates down on the table.

"That's strange," said Fern, and gave Aunt Twyla Mrs. Coney's apologetic message. But Twyla sniffed.

"No more than she ought. They caught the two boys who upset Coney's tubs. Cops found 'em kicking over litter bins, brought them into the station for questioning, and one of them blew the gaff on the other. Nasty little scum—I hope they get sent to preventive."

"Oh, I'm glad," said Fern. "Then—" She was beginning to say, "Then no one can go on thinking you did it—" but changed her mind and said instead, "Perhaps they were the ones that broke your windows."

"*Perhaps*—" said Aunt Twyla sourly.

After supper she remarked, "It's odd. I keep thinking I can hear somebody upstairs. I must be going daft in my old age."

"Maybe it's the pylon humming," said Fern uneasily. For no particular reason, she added, "When does Uncle Frank next come home?"

"Not for another six weeks. I think I'll go to the phonebooth on the corner and ring up to ask after your mother. You'd best go to bed."

"I'll wait up till you come back," said Fern. She felt very reluctant to get undressed and lie under the covers in the dark, in her tiny box bedroom with its window looking toward the pylon and the railway.

She locked herself in the bathroom, ran the tap to drown the hum of the pylon, brushed her teeth for a very long time, washed her face over and over, then came out, hoping that Aunt Twyla would be home already, that she would have better news—

The lights were off in the front room, but the passage one, still on, threw some light in each direction. Fern felt a draft, and, over the smell of soap and toothpaste, caught another smell—sharp, strong, choking. She walked into the front room and a dark, bulky figure, suddenly unbent from something it had been doing low down, knocked against the corner of the table and let out a hoarse, frightened cry. Fern heard a mighty whoosh! like the bark of an enormous dog, a sheet of flame swept across the room, and tablecloth, chaircovers, curtains all caught fire together.

Fern, not far from the back door, ran for it, then spun around, thinking crazily, "Alice! I must get Cousin Alice out!"

But the front room was already a dazzling cave of gold and scarlet flame; nobody was going to come out of there. Fern ran into the pitch-dark garden and cannoned into somebody—a man; she let out a yelp as he grabbed her, demanding, "Is that the girl? Are you all right? Thank God! Oh, thank God! But your aunt—where is she?"

"She went to phone—she'll be in front—"

It was Mr. Coney.

What in the world was he doing here?

Before they could get around to the front, they saw something terrible—a flaming creature that raced across the garden, howling, flung itself through the rickety fence, and collapsed on the ground between the pylon's huge legs, rolling and moaning, "Help me! Help me!"

"Ozzie!" screamed Mr. Coney.

Another figure ran after the first carrying a bundle

of something dark and thick, which it flung over the burning, rolling creature—then knelt and thumped, beat, thumped again, pressing out the flames. Mr. Coney ran to help, ducking under the pylon, taking no notice of the DANGER signs.

"Is that you, Mrs. Deane?" Fern heard him gasp.

And heard Aunt Twyla's dour reply, "Whom did you expect? Cinderella? Take a hand with this groundsheet, Bob Coney."

Fire engines had arrived at the front of the house, which by now was burning so hard that there seemed no possible chance of saving it. All the firemen could do was play their hoses around and stop the fire from spreading to the timber yard or the pylon.

An ambulance carried away Ozzie Coney, who was severely burned. His clothes reeked of gasoline, and an empty petrol can was found at the starting point of the fire. A police officer traveled with Ozzie in the ambulance.

"If it hadn't been for Mrs. Deane and her groundsheet, your son would be dead," he had told Mr. Coney, who looked terrible, Fern observed—shocked, wretched, suddenly an old man.

"I don't know what to say," he muttered to Aunt Twyla. "You saved him—how can I thank you? I—I only hope you don't think Mary and I egged him on to do this awful thing—?"

"Well, I don't," said Aunt Twyla, roundly and surprisingly. "I've thought plenty hard things of you in the past, Bob Coney, but I never thought you'd take a hand in *arson.*"

"He was bumbling away after tea, talking to himself, something about Crossing Cottage and then the fuel for the mower. It was only later I suddenly put two and two together, guessed what he might have in mind, and came hell for leather after him. The poor daft boy got a notion in his head you'd had a hand in our Sue's illness."

Aunt Twyla laughed shortly as she turned to watch her house burning.

"If I'd got the powers some folks credit me with, I'd be able to stop this, eh?"

They stood in silence for a moment or two, looking at the roaring flames. Behind them the pylon shone like a scarlet brooch against the black sky.

"I'd best be away to the hospital," said Mr. Coney at length. "See to my poor stupid boy. But Mary said, Mrs. Deane—if anything happened—would you and your niece come and put up at our house, we've beds for you both—"

"Oh," she said, "but you've a sick young one—"

"No, Sue's made the turn, Leigh says, just this evening, she's out of danger; that's why I feel so terrible, what that boy of ours did. *Please,* Mrs. Deane—Mary wouldn't take no for an answer."

"Then we'll say thank you, and kindly. Come along, Fern. One thing," said Aunt Twyla with rare cheerfulness, "we've naught to carry but ourselves." And indeed she walked along Brewery Way and Gasworks Road as lightly as if she had tossed aside a whole lifetime's load of heavy luggage.

Fern had something to carry; she had picked it up off the front path as they left, something that shone in the firelight and caught her eye.

"What do you think this is, Aunt Twyla?" she asked, as they reached the brighter lights of the High Street.

"That? Let's see. Why—no! *I don't believe it!*" whispered Twyla.

She stared at the thing in Fern's hand as if her eyes were still dazzled by the fire, stung by the smoke, and could hardly see what lay in front of them. It was a small mother-of-pearl fish, with an ivory-and-silver ring attached to it and a white satin ribbon tied to the ring.

"It belonged to Alice," whispered Twyla. "It was her teething ring."

Alice.

For the first time since the fire Fern fetched up the courage to ask, "Aunt Twyla? Did you get through to the hospital? Is there—"

"They said she'll be all right," said Twyla slowly. "Just this evening she opened her eyes, quite sensible, and asked for a cup of tea."

Mrs. Coney welcomed them in, couldn't do enough for them. She gave them hot drinks laced with sherry, lent them nightwear, put hot-water bottles in two beds side by side in her spare bedroom. Sue, she said, was getting perkier all the time; and Bob had phoned from Haleswick Hospital to say that although Ozzie's burns were very bad—he'd been taken off to a special Burns Center —he would probably pull through.

"I don't know how to tell you how bad I feel about your house, Mrs. Deane. Our poor backward boy—I'm bound to say—I do blame ourselves too. He grew up among people thinking hard thoughts, hearing hard words spoken. We'll try to put that right now."

"There's been fault on both sides," said Aunt Twyla.

"One thing Bob did say—did you know the house next door is coming up for sale?"

"Let's hope the insurance money will stretch to cover it," said Aunt Twyla. And she did a thing she had not done, perhaps for years, thought Fern; she smiled.

"We'd best get to bed. Thank you, Mary; it's been a long day."

Safe in bed, sandwiched with hot-water bottles, Fern murmured, "Good night, Aunt Twyla." And wondered if Twyla and her mother would be sharing dreams tonight.

"Sleep well, Fern." After a moment Twyla said, "My daughter Alice's little room was just the other side of this wall."

Cousin Alice, thought Fern. Good night, Cousin Alice. Sleep well. You'll be glad to be back in your own home again. You'll rest better there.

The Legacy

WHEN PAUL FOX bought the house called the Legacy, he reckoned that he had acquired a rare bargain. True, the house, a large, plain eighteenth-century mansion that had stood empty for fifteen years, was derelict and in need of total renovation; but the stone outer wall and massive tiled roof were sound, the garden, if neglected, was large, and the house was within easy walking distance of the town center. And Spyre Market was a charming little place, half town, half village, bustling with antique shops, only just beginning to be taken notice of by the developers. Paul felt sure that in the Legacy he had an excellent investment. Refurbish the house, put the garden in order, and in a few years he could sell at a huge profit. Meanwhile he'd live there himself and use the place as a base for a bit of antique dealing; not a shop (the terms of the purchase precluded that) but some gentlemanly viewing and overseas sales to transatlantic or Japanese customers. Antique furniture always looked twice as desirable when observed in a home setting with roses outside the window and so forth.

Accordingly the Legacy was set in order; local builders were not available, but Fox brought in Joliffe's, a firm that he had used before for similar jobs, from the county town twenty miles away.

As to why such an eligible house had stood empty for so long, until the attic floor fell straight through to the cellar, Fox did not particularly inquire, nor did anybody come forward to proffer information. The former owners had been eccentrics, he vaguely gathered, had laid some sort of injunction that the place was to be left empty, and it took a long time for this legal barrier to be done away with; they had been a very odd pair, had no telephone for fear of disturbing the birds, for the same reason kept a mailbox up at the top of the drive, so postmen need not come down to the house, ate only canned food, for which they shopped once a month, and were hardly ever seen about the town. Nobody who was still around seemed to have known them intimately.

The only person, Fox gathered, who might be able to tell him anything about this couple, the Batesons, currently lay at death's door in the local Cottage Hospital. He was a Commander Marchbanks, now in his nineties, father of the present attorney general and grandfather of several rising young politicians.

Bearing a bunch of grapes, Fox went to call on the commander. (He never had the least objection to pushing in where angels feared to tread if it was likely to furnish him with information that might be commercially or socially useful.)

The commander, propped against pillows, was certainly an impressive figure. He had a long, distinguished face, a drooping white mustache, and an ironic expression.

"I suppose the Batesons were great gardeners?" suggested Fox politely.

The commander grinned, showing a double row of smoke-stained teeth, all his own. "Oh, no, I wouldn't call them that. No, no . . . I remember once when Charley Bateson sawed off the branch he had his ladder propped against. . . . No, they were certainly no great shakes as gardeners."

"Why were they so hermitlike in their habits?"

"Oh—" said the old man vaguely. "One is as one grows older, don't you know? There aren't so many people one cares to be acquainted with. All one's real friends are dead. . . ."

He studied his thick-skinned visitor with evident amusement.

"Is it true that Mrs. Bateson died in the garden?"

"Yes, perfectly true. She survived Charley by a couple of years. First she ran him over—"

"Ran him over?"

"Backing the car, in the dark, don't you know, so as to get through the narrow gate. Lots of wives run over their husbands," the old man remarked with his grin. "Accidental death, it was brought in, of course. She went on living there alone, but after a bit she took up residence in the Angel Hotel. Only went to the house by daylight, to feed the birds and so forth. Then one morning she was found on a bench in the garden. I found her, 's a matter of fact. Her expression was quite calm. Well," he corrected himself, "moderately calm. She'd never been back to the Angel the previous night. Natural causes, they brought in, that time. Well, everything's natural, in a manner o' speaking, ain't it?" He grinned again. "Moved in yet, have ye? Comfortable, is it, there? Devilish *un*comfortable in the Batesons' day, it was—ghastly bad taste they had; all Benares trays and potted palms. Heh, heh, heh! Still, he had a very sound taste in port, did old Charley. Put the garden in order yet, have ye?"

"It's a terrible job. The brambles were rooted six feet deep—"

"Trouble with moles, you're bound to have too. The Batesons always had shocking trouble with moles. Well, well, well! Thanks for the grapes!"

Fox gathered that the audience was dismissed.

And when he would have gone back next week, to ask the old boy's view about a really interesting discovery, he was told that Commander Marchbanks had died.

"Didn't you see it in the local paper?" said the matron coldly.

But Fox only read the bits about property in the local paper.

The interesting discovery had been made by the builders.

Commander Marchbanks, Fox rapidly realized, had been absolutely right about the mole problem. In among the huge blackberry thickets, wherever space availed, there were whole colonies of monumental molehills and runways. The only thing to do if one wanted a decent lawn, which Fox certainly did, was to dig up the whole area in front of the house and cover it, half an inch deep, with strong metal mesh. No mole could fight its way upward through that; if they chose to burrow underneath it, that was their affair. But presumably, in an area several hundred yards square, the moles would, by and by, if they were unable to surface, die from lack of air.

So the site was excavated. Up came the bramble roots, deep and knobbed, and thick yellow mats of nettle roots. Up came old bits of broken china; half bricks; mysterious, rusty portions of old garden tools; and window fastenings.

And, in the middle of the area, a stone slab was revealed.

Here lyes the bodie of Samuel Fych, dyed in his sinnes 1612, it said unequivocally.

Paul Fox was really sorry that the old commander was not still around to offer suggestions about this interesting find. For the annals of the town were completely mute and blank as to the identity or history of Samuel Fych; nor were the county archives of any greater help. Local historians were interested but uninformed. And Fox was unable to discover anything useful in the history of the house; it had been built comparatively recently, only two hundred years ago, on the site of an earlier structure. But what that had been nobody was able to tell him.

Meanwhile what to do about the slab? It was a nuisance, lying just where it did; the builders would either have to prise it up or cut an oblong gap in the mole-proof mesh to accommodate it—which would destroy the whole purpose of the mesh. If the moles could get through at that point, they would soon be burrowing about all over the place.

"Oh, take it up, take it up!" said Paul at last impatiently. "You can set it, upright, in the garden wall where it's crumbling badly; that's what they do in graveyards when they turn them into parks."

The garden was surrounded by high stone walls, all

crumbling to some degree; the stone slab looked very well, set vertically in one of them and cleaned up a bit. Fox forgot to inquire whether the builders had dug down, at all, under where the slab had lain, but assumed they had not, as nobody made any further allusion to the matter.

The builders were an excellent firm and had done several previous jobs for Fox; but he never remembered one where they had whipped through a piece of renovation with such remarkable speed; all the work was completed between March and the end of September. It was as if they wanted to leave the site before the shorter evenings began. One young bricklayer in fact was heard to say something about "not fancying it in that cellar much," but he was soon paid off and sent about his business. "Not a good workman," the boss said. "Casual. Slipshod."

On the day Fox moved into the house, he taped an interview with the local TV station. (He had friends, or at least acquaintances, in all kinds of handy quarters, well placed to receive or pass on news as to possible business deals.) The two useful minutes on the local network admiringly described and displayed the sympathetic restoration that had been carried out, mentioned the possibility of a Heritage Award for the work, congratulated Mr. Fox on having rescued the derelict house for his own private occupation, not just for vulgar profit (or not just yet at any rate) and, to conclude, mentioned the interesting memorial stone that had been discovered. "If any of our viewers can throw light on this find," the announcer said, "we, or Mr. Fox, will be glad to hear from them." And then passed on to the horrible results of an oil spill on the local beaches.

The first week or so of Fox's occupancy was spent

in arranging a carefully chosen consignment of appropriate furniture. Nothing too antique—a bit of Hepplewhite, some good rugs of course, minor watercolors on the walls, a print or two, chinaware in the kitchen, and a nice French country table. Fox did notice that the newly installed central heating creaked a great deal, but that was bound to be so, at first, the builders assured him, in a building where, of necessity, all the woodwork was brand new. (The old woodwork had had to be burned. It was past even using for firewood.) Also, when the wind was in the north, as it mostly seemed to be, the double glazing on the windows and draft-proofing around the doors let out extraordinary banshee screeches and mumbles; the screeches Paul found he could tolerate better than the mumbles, which sounded exactly like a petulant half-wit continually maundering away to himself.

A telephone had been installed (with none of the usual delay) and a TV set and aerial delivered; Paul had stipulated that the latter should be supplied in time for him to watch his own recorded interview, which, when it was screened, seemed to him (as is so often the case) remarkably short, shallow, and scrappy.

After the screening, however, several neighbors recognized and congratulated him in the street, and about two nights later the telephone rang.

"—Hallo?" said Fox, who had not yet memorized his new number.

"Saw you on TV!" drawled a faint, mocking voice —this was a long-distance call, evidently, interrupted by a lot of static. For all its broken and muffled quality, the voice was vaguely familiar. Could it be that of Commander Marchbanks? But no, he was dead of course. It was the slightly derisive tone that had re-called the old man.

"Nice thing you've made of the house—very nice," the voice said amid crackles. "All right if I drop in one evening?"

"Of course, come in for a drink," said Fox automat-ically—this might be a potential customer—"but—for-give me—I didn't catch your name?"

Now, however, the voice vanished completely, and Fox was left with a dead line. Irritably he replaced the receiver—still, if he was interested, the chappie would phone again—and went back to the television set. This, as the installing engineer had prophesied, was suffering from what he had called teething troubles. That is, any picture tended to dissolve into swimming blankness. Twiddling the controls for ten minutes together, Fox could achieve nothing but a kind of cylindrical dark shape in the middle of the screen, which occasionally almost formed itself into a human image approaching, then receded again into a blurred distance.

Get back TV engineer, scribbled Paul on his list of things to be done. *Have draft-proofing retested*—for the banshee scream and maniac murmur were even worse and were beginning to get him down. Also the boards through which heating pipes ran continually clicked as if giant death-watch beetles were munching them; but there was nothing to be done about that. *Get more mole bombs.* Paul wrote. For the moles, deprived of their playground in front of the house, were deter-minedly tunneling along each side of the metal mesh, raising a molehill every meter or so, seemingly bent on boring their way under the house itself. Paul buried barbed wire, broken glass, holly prickles, and gorse branches in their runways (following the advice of different experts), but the only things that seemed to slow them down at all were the smoke bombs, which, when lit and tucked into the burrows, evoked spurts of black smoke from all over the ground; evidently the network of runways was as complicated as it was well established. After a vigorous treatment with these, the moles would stay quiet for a few days, regrouping perhaps.

Meanwhile, indoors, Paul had observed a queer thing.

At the head of the brand-new staircase he had caused to be inserted a large new window, giving light along both the upstairs and downstairs hallways. This window faced east; sometimes the sun shone through it, sometimes the moon. At these times, walking downstairs, Paul would see his own shadow thrown ahead of him.

But twice, lately, approaching the head of the stairs along the right-angled upper hall, glancing over the banisters, he had seen a man's shadow cast down the staircase *before* he himself had reached the stair.

As if somebody were standing outside the window looking in. Which was preposterous, for it was on the second floor, eighteen feet above ground.

Then, of course, Fox himself reached the top of the stairs and there was his own shadow, obscuring the other one. And running down rather quickly, he tried to put the odd phenomenon out of his mind. It was probably, must be, an optical illusion.

It would be pleasant, he thought, to get somebody, some friend, to come and stay for a few days. After all, the Legacy was rather a large house to occupy on one's own.

But all his friends seemed to be out of town, or out

of sorts, or out of touch. It was surprising how one did lose touch with people after a year or two.

Another very odd thing was the habit the TV had of coming on all by itself. He would walk into the lounge, and immediately his eye would be caught by the eerie glimmer of the bluish, pearly screen, with that vague, dark, indeterminate shape in the middle—like a person's body all wrapped up in bandages. He was certain that he'd switched the set off.

Fox took to pulling out the plug and antenna cord when he left the room; but just the same, when he returned, three times out of four the set would be switched on again. No sound: just the vague, trembling image.

Doorbell was another note that he scribbled on his list of things to be done. The builders, curse them, after having been all over the place, hammering away, week after week, until he longed to see them leave, had now vanished without a trace leaving a maddening legacy of small unfinished items and little faults that needed putting right. *"Legacy,"* thought Fox. Ha! very appropriate. There was this bell, for example; the same bell rang, in the middle of the house, for both front- and back-door buttons, a good loud bell, since Fox was somewhat hard of hearing.

But, due to an electrical fault somewhere, presumably, it would ring two or three times a day with that irritating loud buzz when there was no person at either door. Paul would hurry from one entrance to the other —but no, there was not a soul to be seen.

That must definitely be dealt with.

He took to locking his bedroom door at night. A ridiculous, old-maidish habit—but the house did stand somewhat isolated, and there had been several burglaries recently. Now the village was becoming such a known center of the antiques trade; this precaution was, he felt, only sensible.

So it was particularly demoralizing, one morning, to get up and find that the shoes he had worn the previous evening stood where he had left them the night before, neatly aligned in front of the bedroom radiator, and were, both of them, stuffed as tight as they could hold with the foil tops off milk bottles. *Crammed* with the things! What could you make of that? Some people saved foil bottle tops and strung them on strings as bird scarers, but Fox had never done so. He threw them out with the rubbish, never had more than a couple in the kitchen. So where the *devil* had all those come from? And who had stuffed them all into his shoes? In a locked room? In the middle of the night?

And—more unnerving still—when Fox went to open the bedroom door, he found that the key was missing. Not in the lock, not to be found anywhere. Mercifully—for his predicament might otherwise have been quite serious, no one these days came near the house for days together—he had a complete set of spare house keys in his bureau drawer, which the—which whoever had played this singularly pointless and silly practical joke must not have known about—so he was able to let himself out and go down to imbibe a breakfast that consisted entirely of Irish coffee. Fox was becoming rattled. And more so, when, glancing up at his charmingly arranged kitchen dresser, with all the willow pattern and Lowestoft, he saw that, up on the top shelf, crammed between two beautiful blue and white Chinese ginger jars, leaned a massive dirty old pewter meat cover, which had *certainly* not been there the night before.

He climbed on a chair, lifted it down, and surveyed it with indignant disgust. Whoever put it there might have washed it before doing so! It was still covered in traces of earth, as if just dug up. An empty snail shell adhered to the undersurface. No doubt it might fetch a fair enough price as old pewter, but it was quite *rudely* out of place among his carefully chosen chinaware— which begged the question of who, *who*, had set it up there between last night and this morning? Was it some practical joker among the builders who had retained a key to the house? The lad who had been sacked for bad workmanship perhaps?

But Joliffe, the head of the building firm, when finally run to ground by phone on a far-distant site, disclaimed all knowledge of extra house keys. Mr. Fox had been handed all five, he said; there were no more. And anyway young Andy Heather could not have played the joke; he was in jail, serving five days for drunkenness and disorder. The pranks—harmless enough, they sounded—must have been perpetrated by some of Mr. Fox's friends. And Joliffe excused himself quickly, before Fox could raise the matter of the doorbell, the draft proofing, and the cellar door, which would never stay closed. Continually came open with a loud click.

I'll go up to London for the weekend, Fox decided. Leave early tomorrow morning. And I'll put the house on the market, quietly. Take a loss on it, but never mind. No sense in staying here with all this bother. Something (he did not put it more specifically than that), something is just trying to make it inconvenient for me to stay here. Inconvenient! It makes Borley Rectory seem like the Hilton. Well—I can take a hint. I'll leave tomorrow morning. Early.

Rinsing his coffeepot, he looked through the window over the kitchen sink, and started, almost dropping the jug. For a moment he thought he had seen the same swaddled shape that showed on the TV screen, only outside the window now, peering in.

But then of course with relief he remembered that it was the new little, well-grown cypress tree that he had planted there yesterday, dripping quietly out there in the October mist. Nothing worse than that. It was quite shaming how a few odd, unrelated incidents could make you jumpy in your nerves.

Fox would have liked to go out for the day, over to an antique-dealers' fair that was being held at Sanditon; but unfortunately he had to wait there for the inspector from the Gas Board, who was due to come that day to inspect all the installations.

After the manner of his kind, this individual did not turn up until half past five in the evening, so there was the day wasted. Even more annoying, when Fox was down in the cellar with the inspector looking at the gas boiler, the phone rang. Fox raced up the cellar stairs, but got there too late, and there was no message on the answering machine, though the button glowed red; only the word "Wait" abruptly cut off. So many people were still absurdly put off by these useful devices, could think of nothing sensible to say.

The gas inspector, having given his okay to the place, was invited by Fox to have a drink. Fox indeed made quite a point of it, but the man said no thanks, he had to get home, his wife would have dinner waiting. So Fox walked him to his van.

"Trouble with moles, I see," the man remarked as he backed on the turnaround.

The lines of hillocks had almost reached the house now.

Fox debated eating out at a pub, but the thought of returning to the empty, dark house was a deterrent; he decided to make himself a frozen TV dinner and turn in early.

In his bath, after having carried out this program, he noticed that the wind was rising; the gauze bathroom curtain suddenly billowed inward on a wild flapping curve.

But how could it do that when the window was not only closed but double glazed?

Fox, locking his bedroom door, putting the key in his pajama pocket, heard, downstairs, the cellar door click open again.

A moment later, under the covers by now, he heard a slow, heavy step ascending the stairs.

Fox's body, like that of Mrs. Bateson, was found on a seat outside in the garden.

But unlike Mrs. Bateson, his expression was not even moderately calm.

The house known as the Legacy is again up for sale.

About the Author

The distinguished English writer Joan Aiken is the author of over fifty books for young readers and twenty-five novels for adults. Her juvenile list includes the Wolves Chronicles, featuring the intrepid Dido Twite and her friends. Her collections of stories of the supernatural include *Give Yourself a Fright*, *A Touch of Chill*, and *A Whisper in the Night*. Her most recent novel for Delacorte Press was *Return to Harken House*, the story of a visit to a haunted house.

Joan Aiken is the daughter of Conrad Aiken. She lives in Sussex, England.